RACHEL
HAIMOWITZ

ANCHORED

BELONGING

'VERSE

RIPTIDE
PUBLISHING

Riptide Publishing
PO Box 6652
Hillsborough, NJ 08844
www.riptidepublishing.com

Anchored

Cover Art by Tami Santarossa, http://lillilolita.deviantart.com/
Editors: Sarah Frantz
Cover Design, and Layout: L.C. Chase, lcchase.com/design.htm

ISBN: 978-1-62649-236-3

Second edition
September, 2014

Also available in ebook:
ISBN: 978-1-62649-235-6

RACHEL
HAIMOWITZ

ANCHORED

BELONGING
'VERSE

RIPTIDE
PUBLISHING

To Bill O'Reilly, for the loofah.

TABLE OF
CONTENTS

PROLOGUE

TWENTY-FIVE YEARS EARLIER

Daniel was folding ties for a new display when a well-dressed man knocked on the door of the boutique. They were appointment only, and he knew this man didn't have one because the mistress was out to lunch and she *never* missed appointments. But if he turned away potential business, she'd be mad. She'd beat him.

Daniel sighed and put down a tie midfold. She'd probably beat him for letting the man in, too. He wasn't supposed to wait on customers, after all—he was only eleven, and good for nothing anyway—but his mom was two blocks over picking up buttons, and Jaime was delivering a suit uptown, which meant it was him or no one.

The man knocked again. Daniel straightened his own tie, ran a careful hand over his hair, and went to the door. He thought of saying, *I'm sorry, we're closed, sir*, but the man looked made of money, and Daniel couldn't risk him complaining. He unlocked the door.

"Welcome to Roberta's, sir," Daniel managed to say without stuttering. Like Jaime would do, or the mistress, all smooth and confident. "Do you have an appointment?"

The man looked at him, looked at him in a way he'd only recently begun to understand, and Daniel darted his eyes to the floor, throat tightening, stinging. They were alone here, no one to stop the man from . . . But he *wouldn't*, would he? Wouldn't touch someone else's property without their permission. Wouldn't *damage* it like that. It was against the law. Men dressed as nice as this man didn't break the law, did they?

"I'm afraid not," the man said, voice gentle, and Daniel dared a glance up from his polished shoes. The man was smiling. A nice smile—not at all like the way those other customers had smiled before they'd . . . before they'd *hurt* Daniel. "Do I need one?"

Daniel swallowed down the tightness in his throat and said to the man's silver belt buckle, "The mistress is at lunch, sir."

"Then maybe *you* can help me until she returns. That would please her, wouldn't it?"

Daniel meant to say yes—*Never contradict a customer, you useless little shit!*—but his body had other ideas, and he ended up half nodding, half shaking his head all at once.

"Let me see your face, boy." The man took hold of Daniel's chin, but not rough like his mistress, and Daniel dared to let his eyes stray all the way up to the man's clean-shaven upper lip. He held perfectly still, didn't even tremble, though he knew there was no way this could end well. The mistress would come in and find them like this and she'd be *so mad* and then—

And then the magic question, the one his mistress, in her endless stream of beatings and berating, had told him he would never, ever hear: "Are you for sale, boy?"

"I'm difficult, sir," he replied, just like he'd been trained. "You wouldn't want me. Nobody wants me."

The man smiled, stroked Daniel's face with a gentleness so startling that Daniel nearly jumped, and then pulled the hem of Daniel's fitted shirt from his pants.

Daniel's heart sank even as it began to thrash against his ribs. He'd told the man the truth, answered the way he'd been taught. Would the stranger punish him for that? Or worse, use him the way the mistress had recently let some of her other customers do while they waited for their suits? He glanced once, frantically, around the small showroom floor, hoping his mistress might magically appear. But no—even if she were to return from lunch right now, she would not protect him if this man felt wronged. She would watch, most likely, and then beat him later herself for upsetting a customer, and send him to bed without supper again.

The man spun him around, and Daniel swallowed hard, squeezed his eyes closed. He wouldn't run, and he wouldn't beg, and he wouldn't cry. Running and begging just made things worse, and crying was for babies.

But there was no pain, and no move to undress him further. Only a sigh, low and deep, and a heavy hand on his shoulder. "Relax, boy," the man said, "I won't hurt you." The last man to strip Daniel had said the same thing, and it'd been a lie. A terrible, *terrible* lie. "I just want to see how difficult your mistress thinks you are."

Daniel believed him. Or maybe he just really, really wanted to. Either way, the muscles in Daniel's shoulder hesitantly unclenched beneath the man's touch. The man released him and lifted Daniel's shirt. Cool air met his back, and then fingertips skimmed a line of welts, gentle enough to be painless. A tug on the waistband of his pants sent his heart jackhammering again—to Daniel's horror, he actually took half a step forward, like his stupid body didn't realize how *bad* and *wrong* it was to try to escape his duties. But the man only lowered his waistband an inch or two, and then more feather touches traveled along the marks high on his hips, on the curve of his buttocks. The man let out a low whistle and spun Daniel back around.

"Quite difficult indeed, eh? Well, you'd better put yourself back together before your mistress sees you." The man's face looked carefully blank—no anger, no impatience, none of that *other* thing, either—but his eyes, Daniel thought, were smiling just a little. "And then show me something in a dark gray chalk stripe."

The mistress looked shocked, then angry, when she came back from lunch to find Daniel tucking and pinning the man's suit for alterations, but before she could work up too big a head of steam, the man said, "Sorry I didn't make an appointment, but Daniel here was very helpful." He fished his wallet from the pants draped across the table beside the stool he was standing on, pulled out his credit card, and then waved to himself. "I'd like to buy this, please. Daniel said he wasn't allowed to use the register."

Daniel knew better than to think the mistress's anger was defused, but of course she wouldn't show it in front of a happy customer. He went back to pinning the man's pants. The mistress ran his charge card, all the while apologizing profusely for not being here, for any unknown slights her stupid slave might've committed while she was gone, for not having offered him a refreshment the moment she walked in. He waved her off, promised he'd been well cared for, but it wouldn't matter. It never did. Not even the four-thousand-dollar sale would matter. The moment the customer was out the door, the mistress would punish Daniel just the same.

Or so he was convinced, anyway, until the man took back his credit card, pointed it at Daniel, and said, "I'd like to buy this too, please."

Daniel jolted so hard he almost stuck the man with a pin. *Not possible*, he thought, and then, *But what about my mom?* and then, *Oh God now you* have *to take me you can't leave me here*, when he saw the cold fury twisting his mistress's face.

"He's a lousy fuck," she said.

Daniel was staring resolutely at the man's shoes, but he could picture the gentleness on the man's face, hear it in his voice when he said, "That's not why I want him."

"Then why?" the mistress practically spat. She'd kept the checkout counter between her and them, but now she circled around, big angry steps, and what had happened to *never contradict a customer*?

The man stepped off the stool, met her halfway. Daniel kept his head down and busied his hands with his pins and chalk and measuring tape, but his entire focus was on the man and his mistress. He might be nothing but a dumb cunt slave, but even *he* knew how important this was. How much his life might be about to change. How much his *mother's* might change if he had to leave her alone here, couldn't protect her anymore. His hands stilled—no one was paying him any attention anyway—and he watched them through his lashes, breath held.

"Allow me to introduce myself," the man said, and stuck his hand out for the mistress to shake. He seemed so *pleasant*, even in the face of her wary, guarded anger. But he was a customer, after all, so she took his hand. "I'm William Krantz. The Chief VP of Human Resources over at NewWorld Media."

The name meant nothing to Daniel, but it obviously meant something to the mistress, whose mean mouth turned up in the kind of grin she reserved for *stupid rich fucks born to be parted with their money, and if you ever repeat that I'll beat you to death, do you hear me?* Then she turned that dangerous smile on Daniel, who dropped his gaze so quickly he made himself dizzy for a second. "Go to your room, Daniel."

Never in all his life had he found it so difficult to make his mouth say, "Yes, Mistress," what with the panic all tangled up with excitement clawing through his throat. But he managed it somehow, and through the same magic got his feet moving to obey. He scurried through the shop into the back room, then up the narrow flight of stairs and down the short hall to the bunkroom he shared with his mom and Jaime.

And then, like the bad little slave he was, he crawled beneath the bunk bed and pressed his ear to the air vent.

But they must've been sitting by the wet bar, which was all the way across the store from his room, because he couldn't make out a thing. Still, he stayed there, breath held and trying to still his noisy heart, for a good two or three minutes. Until the thought of the mistress coming up and finding him sneaking like this scared him more than the outcome of their conversation, and he wormed out from under the bed. He must not've cleaned well enough under there this week, because some dust specked the knees of his dress pants, but he wiped it off easily enough. Then sat down on the lower bunk—the one he still shared with his mom because the room wasn't big enough for a cot and it beat sleeping in the smaller upper bed with Jaime—and just tried to *breathe*. To reason.

If the man didn't want him to fuck, then why *did* he want him? All he knew was tailoring and housework, so what could he possibly do for the man, who was wealthy and surely already had all the house slaves he could possibly need? Daniel crossed his hands in his lap and fiddled with the braided steel bands welded on each wrist. They were getting tight. He'd need new ones soon. If the man bought Daniel, might he have any use for Daniel's mother too? *She* was a good fuck—he heard it all the time from the mistress's best clients. And she could clean and sew and cook and even dance, dance as beautifully as those freewomen in pretty pink leotards in the old New York City Ballet program she'd kept from since before he was born.

But she was getting old now, thirty-six this March, and what would a rich man want with an old dancing slave?

Daniel stared out the window overlooking the old brownstone's ventilation shaft and realized he was crying.

No. *No.* Crying was for babies, and he was a man now. He *was.* Man enough to service customers in private. Man enough to be sold on with or without his mom.

But please, God, with. I don't ask you for much, I'm just a slave with no soul, I know that, and I know I don't feel what real people feel and I know I can't love like real people love, but please, God. Please. *She's all I've got.*

But God didn't listen, of course He didn't, His mercy wasn't for abominations like Daniel, for slaves, for those born soulless and wrong. People like Daniel could only hope to earn God's love through good, loyal service, and no matter how hard he tried, he'd never quite seemed to manage that in his mistress's eyes.

So it came as no surprise when she called him downstairs, and his mother wasn't there, and nobody even mentioned her as the businessman bundled up his new suit and his new slave and put them both in the backseat of a sleek, black sedan. The man's driver—a valued slave, Daniel could see, from the fine gold chains around both wrists, which could never be used to restrain the man like Daniel's could—pulled the car away without a word. Away from the only owner he'd known for the entirety of his eleven years, and she'd sold him without a single word, a single glance. Just a cheery exchange of papers for money and a too-hard slap on the back.

He tried not to fidget or cry in the backseat of his new master's car, wanting desperately to look around, wanting his mother even more desperately. But he didn't dare ask about her or unglue his eyes from his feet. His master was sitting next to him, watching him so intently that Daniel felt the heat of the man's stare. He wouldn't cry in front of this man. He *wouldn't cry.*

"Daniel?" the man said, and the "Yes, sir?" rolled so instinctively off his tongue that he had to stop, correct himself, say, "Yes, Master," instead. And didn't that feel strange, because his mistress's husband had died so long ago that he couldn't even remember the man's face.

"I'm not your master," the man said in that same kind, patient tone he'd used all along, and at that, Daniel couldn't help but look up, a question in his eyes that he thought for sure would be slapped or punched clean away. And then he'd *really* cry, he wouldn't be able to help it anymore. But the man just smiled and said, "I bought you for NewWorld Media. Do you know who they are?"

Daniel swallowed hard. "No, sir." He started to apologize for being such a dumb cunt slave, but the man just kept on talking.

"What about InfoGlobe? Do you know what that is?"

Daniel nodded—of course he knew what InfoGlobe was. His mistress would watch in the back room on slow afternoons, letting it drone on while she sewed. Daniel would steal glances whenever he could, enthralled by the wonder of a whole wide world beyond the walls he knew, the limited sights he'd seen. He'd actually gotten so lost once in a report from the front lines of some distant war, filed by a slave—an actual slave reporter!—that his mistress had beaten him bloody for slacking off.

He still thought it might have been worth it.

The businessman reached a hand out, and Daniel bit his lip, wondering how he'd angered the man to violence without even speaking. But the man just ruffled his hair and chuckled again. "Well, NewWorld Media owns InfoGlobe, and now they own you. Because you, my boy, have a face just made for television."

CHAPTER ONE

Now

"**D**aniel, you're late," Tim said from the open door of Daniel's office. He threw a warning glance at his watch and added, "News is *live*, you know."

"Sorry. Coming." Daniel saved the package he'd been editing for tomorrow's broadcast, snatched his jacket and tie, and followed his handler out of his office. No way to tell if Tim would let his tardiness slip or if he'd be paying for it later, but he couldn't afford to worry about that now.

Tim left for the control booth, and Daniel made a dash for the stairs, unwilling to wait for the overworked elevator to take him three floors up to the studio. There wouldn't be time for proper makeup or sound checks then, and he didn't want to get Serena or Mike in trouble.

He trotted into the studio a couple minutes past check-in, breathless and still tying the knot on his tie. Mike handed him his IFB, and the moment he popped the little speaker in his ear, he heard Tim complaining that he looked flushed. Serena must have heard it too, because she came at him with a makeup brush.

"Sound check, Daniel." Tim again, voice sharp through the IFB. Mike was standing patiently behind him, waiting to run the mic wire up the back of his jacket. Daniel flashed an apologetic wince at the camera and stood so Mike could do his thing, winced again when Tim scolded him through the IFB. He liked Tim—liked him a lot, in fact—but Tim had bosses to answer to, and if Daniel screwed up any more tonight, Tim would have to report him.

Stupid, useless cunt.

No. He wasn't that boy anymore. Hadn't been for twenty-five years. Days like this, though, he could still hear her voice so damn clearly, feel her bruising fingers on his chin, her strap on his back.

He shuddered, shook the memory away.

Get it together, Daniel. Right now.

Easier said than done, though. It seemed not even the fear of present-day discipline could turn his thoughts from the issue that'd been gnawing at him all week: his new part-time owner-to-be. Maybe his old owner's voice was so strong today because tonight he'd be calling someone master again for the first time in two and a half decades, and that hadn't exactly been a gleaming highlight of his life. He'd been living in the West Side men's dorm since NewWorld Media had bought him, but tonight . . . Tonight, he'd be sleeping in someone else's home. Someone who'd won the right to be his mistress or master in one of those obscenely expensive celebrity-slave auctions. And Daniel wasn't some ignorant child anymore; he knew there was just one reason why a person would bid six mil for a year's worth of evenings and weekends with him. He'd never once been made to serve like that at NewWorld, but things were clearly changing with the company's debts piling up and share prices dropping, and now hundreds of slaves they'd never used like that before were being leased out to—

". . . iel! Damn it, Daniel!"

Shit. Tim. Daniel tried not to look guilty as he turned to camera 1, cleared his throat, and checked the prompter against the script an intern had dropped on his desk. "Yeah, Tim. I'm uh, I'm sorry, I was—" He cut himself off before any bullshit excuses could fall from his lips and compound the problem. *Maybe a woman won my auction. That wouldn't be so bad, right?* "I'm set. Prompter's set."

"Live in thirty," Tim said, a little stern, a little sad, a lot frustrated. Though he didn't say *Wait for me in your office after the show*, Daniel heard the command anyway.

Great, one more thing to worry about.

Even if he had seen it coming. Even if he did deserve it.

Useless cunt slave.

He wrenched his mind back to the here and now, but still said, "Good evening, my name is Daniel Halstrom, and you're watching

Round the Globe with InfoGlobe," a whole four seconds after they went live.

"Look, buddy," Tim said after the show, with entirely more compassion than Daniel knew what to do with. Daniel stripped off and discarded his suit coat, tie, and dress shirt in short, furious little jerks that would have left his first mistress fainting with horror. "I know you're freaked about tonight, but that's no excuse for what happened in that studio."

"I know." He sighed, stuffing his cuff links in the pocket of his pants before yanking them down.

Tim watched his angry strip show impassively, Daniel's jeans waiting in his outstretched hand.

When Daniel finally managed to work his pants past his shoes, he snatched the jeans with a short, prickly, "Thanks."

"But . . .?" Tim asked, holding out Daniel's T-shirt now.

"But what? But nothing. You may be unusually fine with the whole . . ." he waved a hand between them both ". . . casual thing, but I know better than to make excuses." Daniel grabbed his shirt, turning away from Tim and staying that way as he popped his arms through the sleeves. His hands were trembling; he didn't want Tim to see. "I know you have to tell them. I understand. I'll go downstairs first thing tomorrow, okay? They won't even have to restrain me; I'll be good. Ten hours should be plenty of time to recov—"

Tim touched his shoulder, and Daniel flinched, muscles tense.

"Hey," Tim said softly. "Hey. This is really bothering you, isn't it?"

He didn't dare turn around, lest he look a freeman in the face as he challenged him. "Which part? The imminent torture thing, or the whole being-leased-to-a-stranger-after-twenty-five-years-of-faithful-service thing?" When Tim didn't dignify that with an answer, he tried, "Wouldn't it bother *you*?"

"That's different. I'm not a slave."

In other words: *I feel things like a real boy, Pinocchio. I have a* soul.

Daniel resisted the very strong urge to roll his eyes. He felt *plenty*, thank you very much, and he'd seen enough in his well-traveled, deeply investigative lifetime to have figured out that this God thing was bullshit anyway. Not that he could ever say that to anyone—even liberal left-wing Ivy League Tim went to church every Sunday like clockwork, and not just because he had to be seen there to keep his social standing.

So instead Daniel said, as calmly as he could, "Think about it, Tim. Being leased off to some total stranger who wants God knows what from you—no, worse, God knows *exactly* what. Like I don't do enough for the company already? They've got to strip me of the few moments of peace I ever have? The few moments of free time I'm allowed? They really—"

—expect me to pretend to want this person?

Tim squeezed Daniel's shoulder, but said nothing. The man was rarely speechless, and he respected Daniel enough—slave or no—that maybe he really was listening to what Daniel had to say.

"You're luckier than most, you know," Tim finally said, but it sounded pretty flat to Daniel.

"I know." Daniel nodded. He really *was* lucky, even without that comforting, smothering blanket of faith all the rest of his kind seemed to have. "I just . . . What if they—?"

"NewWorld screened the potential lessors very carefully. Especially those who expressed interest in their most valuable property, of which you most assuredly are. They wouldn't send you to someone who'd mistreat you."

Tim's hand was still on Daniel's shoulder; Daniel shrugged it off and turned to face him. "You mean they wouldn't send me to someone who would mark me in a way that would show on camera," he said, slowly and purposefully blunt. Not everyone was like his old mistress, maybe not even most people, but it wasn't exactly unheard of, and the kind of person who would and could shell out six mil for a lease was either obsessed, dangerous, jealous, or all three. He knew damn well that slaves like him—the ones cursed with good looks, the successful ones who'd accomplished more than most freemen—were magnets for mean crazies like that.

Not to mention that he couldn't fathom why anyone looking for something *normal* would feel inclined to spend six million dollars to get it, even from a famous slave. With that kind of cash, you could outright buy a custom-trained Nevada Arts companion. Two, even, and lily-white both. You didn't need a guy like him.

Daniel bit his lip, but Tim was making that *face* at him, that open, understanding, *tell me what's bothering you* face, and there was no way Daniel could hold the question back: "Why won't you tell me who it is?"

A pause, a grimace; Tim actually looked upset. "The buyer paid us well not to. I'm sorry, Daniel, even *I* don't know who it is. Guess the brass figured you couldn't puppy-dog-eyes it out of me if they didn't tell me. But they *won't hurt you*, Daniel. I promise."

I'm not gonna hurt you, boy. Be a good little cunt now and spread those legs.

Daniel shuddered, half-choking on memories of blood and agony and sobbing so hard he couldn't breathe. *So* not comforting.

Tim grasped Daniel's bare forearms just above the slave bracelets—thin platinum cables bound with rectangular gold links, slim and stunning and masculine without a single ring for binding—and squeezed gently. Daniel looked down at Tim's hands, at his own, at the bracelets so different from the functional iron bands he'd worn twenty-five years ago. No matter his fears, Tim was right; NewWorld Media *had* been good to him. They'd rescued him from cruel oblivion and given him everything. They'd even gone back for his mother, once he'd proven himself a good student, put her to work in wardrobe and never made her—or him—touch another man again. If they wanted him to touch one now in return for those twenty-five amazing years, well . . . then what kind of ungrateful, spoiled little shit was he to balk? He wasn't a child anymore, and surely he'd faced scarier things before, and Tim . . . Tim had never lied to him, not once. He deserved the beating he had coming tomorrow.

"Okay?" Tim asked, hands still on Daniel's arms, studying him closely. "Good?"

Daniel nodded. "Promise you'll pick me up in the morning?"

Tim laughed, grabbed Daniel's coat, and tossed it to him. "Ten on the dot. Don't make the driver come get you."

CHAPTER TWO

The driver was the same one who'd ferried Daniel for the last four years, a quiet, placid giant of a man named Calvin who Daniel had never *once* gotten to talk to him in all the time they'd spent together. He *could* talk—Daniel had heard his occasional "Yes, sir" or "No, sir" or "Ten minutes out, sir" spoken crisply to the dispatcher over the radio. But with Daniel he wouldn't even answer direct questions. Maybe he resented having to serve another slave, especially a white one; sure, they were all part of the same bottom class, but there was no denying his white skin brought privilege even among the low. He could pass for a freeman at first sight; the blacks, the natives, and especially mixes of the two like Calvin couldn't. It certainly wouldn't have been the first time a slave had been jealous of Daniel.

Or maybe those were just Calvin's orders. After all, idle chatter was a sign of idle minds, and a distraction besides, and he'd seen plenty of slaves beaten for less. So he tried not to let it bother him when he asked, "Where to, tonight, Calvin?" and got nothing but silence in return as the car pulled away from the curb.

Daniel stared out the window, too nervous to enjoy this rare glimpse of streets outside his normal route to Hell's Kitchen. They swung up Park Avenue, crossed west on 79th and then turned down Fifth, stopping before a gorgeous pre-war townhome overlooking Central Park. No way one person owned this whole place—it *had* to have been converted to condos, right?

The doorman wore bronze slave bracelets that matched the cuff links on his uniform, and he gave Daniel an abbreviated bow when he opened the door for him. "This way, sir," he said, and didn't that just pull Daniel up short because he was still a slave just like the doorman, no matter the color of his skin or what metal his bands were made of. But Daniel followed him into the lobby—yep, definitely converted; he passed ten mailboxes on the way in, which meant two condos per floor—and the doorman deposited him in the elevator, turned a private key, and pushed the button for the north penthouse. "I'll let him know you're on your way, sir," was the last thing Daniel heard for the next five floors.

Except, of course, for the too-quick *thud-thud-thud* of his own heart in his ears. *Him.* Not a woman, then. A man. With a dick he'd no doubt want to shove places Daniel never wanted to think about again. In fifteen, maybe twenty seconds, Daniel would be meeting the man who'd shelled out *six million dollars* for a year's worth of partial ownership. Over $115,000 a *week* for what'd likely amount to no more than forty waking hours of company. Christ, most top-end companions didn't earn their masters $3,000 an hour, and he hadn't spent his whole life learning how to pleasure people like they had. He'd never even learned how not to bleed all over a man.

Despite Tim's reassurances, there was just no way . . . no way this would be painless. And he had every fucking right to be terrified.

He caught a glimpse of himself in the mirrored panel above the elevator buttons and schooled his face. He couldn't erase the exhaustion, but he was a passable enough actor to clear the fear from his features. He tried on a smile. It didn't fit. Went for neutral instead.

The elevator stopped. Dinged his arrival. He cleared his throat, swallowed hard, threw his shoulders back and forced his hands to unclench at his sides. Forced himself not to fidget. He'd faced down warlords, terrorists, live-fire combat zones, tornadoes, wild dogs . . . surely he could face down *this*.

The door slid open.

Whatever it was he'd thought he might see—old man, young man, old money, new money—it *certainly* wasn't the talk show host who shared his time slot on InfoGlobe's biggest rival network.

Daniel froze.

Stood there.

Forgot how to walk. How to breathe. Even forgot to turn his gaze to the floor, to not look a freeman in the eye. Was this some kind of sick fucking *joke*? Or was fucking him in the ratings not enough for UBC?

Carl Whitman, the charismatic face of UBC's *Whitman Live*— and what a *big* face it was in person, atop an equally big body—smiled down at Daniel like he'd been looking forward to this moment of shock for the last ten years. Daniel thought a greeting might come next, or perhaps a scolding for making eye contact, but instead Carl said, "You're sweating." And then, shit-eating smirk firmly in place, "Come on, before you end up back in the lobby. Lord knows I paid enough for every single second of your time."

Daniel had no memory of walking into Carl's—his *master's*—living room, but there he was, staring obediently at a small patch of ultra-plush off-white carpeting despite the nearly overpowering urge to observe his new surroundings. To observe his *master*—try to figure out exactly what in God's name this whole messed up situation was. Why he was here. Why NewWorld had ever agreed to such a preposterous arrangement, put him in such a perilous position.

But he said nothing, of course. Carl was a freeman; *he* could ask all the questions he wanted. Daniel might've been his equal as a talking head—maybe even his better; he didn't ride a desk all day every day, after all, and he did actual journalism rather than, well, whatever it was that talk show hosts did—but right now, in every way that counted, he was nothing but a slave. Just a slave. And more specifically, *Carl's* slave.

He could feel Carl's gaze raking head to toe, long and appraising, but Carl kept his distance. Yet there was no mistaking the hunger radiating from the man, or the satisfaction—that strange sort of pride only ever seen in freemen, as if they had created rather than simply purchased something impressive.

Finally, after what seemed a long enough stretch to make even the most recalcitrant witness want to spill their guts, Carl spoke. "I saw your show tonight." He sounded far too amused for Daniel's comfort. Was that what this was? Why he'd insisted on the secrecy? Six million dollars to catch his rival by surprise and then humiliate him, and worth every penny?

Carl settled down on a black leather couch with an ease and comfort that Daniel knew he'd never feel anywhere, let alone here. Carl hadn't asked a question or given Daniel permission to speak, so Daniel stayed right where he was, silent and still.

"You looked like a deer caught in headlights all night," Carl said. He chuckled and added, "Still do, actually."

Another pause, where maybe Carl was waiting for him to say something, as if the man didn't know the laws, didn't know how slaves had to behave. Or maybe he just thought of Daniel as different somehow, like the job he did for the men who owned him gave him magical freedoms outside the field or the set.

"You had four seconds of dead air before the lead on your A block." Pause. "My EP would give me ten straight years of shit for that, never let me live it down. What about yours?"

"I'll be punished, Master," Daniel said to his feet, trying to keep his voice strong, to take ownership of his mistake and make it clear that such lapses were neither commonplace nor acceptable in his eyes. That he wasn't a bad slave.

"Take your shirt off. What do you mean, 'punished'?"

The two statements were so disparate that it took Daniel a moment to parse them, and Carl waved a hand and said, "Come on, I've been dying to see what's hiding under the suit and tie since 2008." When Daniel's brow furrowed—*why 2008?*—Carl added, "Chinese earthquake? Nuclear disaster they were pretending so hard wasn't happening? Those soldiers almost killed you trying to scare you out of there. Instead of leaving like sane people, you and your producer hiked through three miles of rubble to find a spot to start broadcasting again."

Ah, that. He actually still had a scar from that particular encounter, a bullet graze on his left triceps he hadn't even felt at the time, he'd been so high on the rush. He bared it as he lifted his T-shirt over his head, hunched in on himself a little once he was topless. He didn't know what to do with the shirt, didn't dare throw it on the floor, so he fisted it in both hands, wringing the fabric nervously.

Carl's eyes were like touches on his skin, a physical weight, pervasive and uncomfortable. "I said," he reminded Daniel, "What do you mean by punished?"

Daniel swallowed hard and forced himself not to hunch up further. "I don't know, Master."

Carl sprang from the couch and crossed the room in two large steps. He tugged the T-shirt from Daniel's hands and tossed it on the couch, ducked his head quite conspicuously to look into Daniel's downturned face, and demanded, "What do you mean, you don't know? They've owned you twenty-five years. Surely this isn't a first."

Daniel swallowed. Did Carl think he was lying? Why on earth would he lie about this? "I don't know how angry they'll be, si—*Master.*" He could've kicked himself for the botched honorific, for the waver in his voice; it wouldn't exactly help his cause if Carl thought he was bullshitting. He cleared his throat, tried to swallow down his fear. "Twenty with the strap, maybe; I need to be able to sit through the broadcast tomorrow night, and to—" *Say it, Daniel. Don't be a coward.* "And to serve you after work, Master."

One giant hand, easily the size of Daniel's whole face, reached out to cup his chin. Carl's thumb traced the line of Daniel's cheekbone from his ear to his nose, and then settled across his lips. "Is that as painful as it sounds?"

Oh God. I was right. He doesn't *want something normal. No wonder he paid so much for me; he's a closet sadist who can't afford to let his secret get out and ruin his career, and who better to get his sick fucking rocks off with than the slave with the audacity to steal his audience share—*

The hand on his chin tightened. "I asked you a question, Daniel."

Daniel nodded, his skin flushing hot beneath the man's touch. "Yes, Master, it is." Maybe Carl would be satisfied with that. Maybe he wouldn't hurt Daniel himself if he knew the folks at NewWorld would be doing a thorough job of it for him.

Carl dropped his hand and stepped away again, then said, "Pants." Again, the change of subject was so abrupt it took Daniel a moment to process. Was Carl going to turn him over his knee and spank him? Fuck him? Both?

Didn't matter. No matter how bad things were about to get, if his old mistress had taught him anything, it was that not obeying would only ever make things worse.

Jaw clenched, he peeled his jeans off.

"Put them on the couch," Carl said. "Socks, underwear, all of it."

Daniel complied with shaking fingers, blushing tip to toe and trembling in the cool air. His hands made a move for pockets that were no longer there, and lest his master think he was trying to hide himself, protect himself from whatever he had coming, he clasped them tightly behind his back.

Carl hovered a few feet away, his expression indecipherable—at least what Daniel could see of it through his downturned gaze. Shrouded hunger, he thought. Tamped eagerness. The face of a man finally getting the one thing he'd always wanted but completely unwilling to let on how much it meant to him.

The silence stretched, stretched some more. Neither of them moved.

Was Carl waiting for him to say something? Do something? The longer the silence, the more dire Daniel's imaginings grew. Not just a spanking, but a belt whipping, a flogging, chains and paddles and leather. Not just a fuck, but a long and torturous run of humiliating words and actions, fingers and cock and toys and tongue and making him beg for it, making him choke, making him lick Carl clean. He'd heard the horror stories from companions back at the dorm, things that'd shocked and broken even those highly trained professionals. He knew what sick shit people were capable of. What Carl might demand of him.

At last, he could bear the waiting no longer and chanced a single word. "Master?"

"Hmm?"

"Should I— I mean, do you ... do you want me to ..."

Daniel had no idea how to finish that sentence, only hoped that maybe, just maybe, if he volunteered something, if he seemed eager, the night might hurt less. But Carl rescued him from his stutterings with another "Hmm," this time more amused than questioning.

"Shower's down the hall on the left," Carl said. "Soap and shampoo in the stall. Fresh towels on the rack. I want you *squeaky* clean, understand?"

"Yes, Master," Daniel said. He understood all too well.

The bathroom was exquisite, all marble counters and heated marble floor tiles and a marble bench in the three-headed marble shower. It was also huge: larger than the entire private dorm room he'd earned as a platinum slave at NewWorld.

Daniel washed quickly but thoroughly, even rubbing a soap-slicked finger over his hole in case his master wanted . . . well, he was trying very hard not to think about that, but better to be prepared than to disappoint the man. The hot spray eased some of the tension from his muscles, and though he longed to stay and enjoy it, stay where he wouldn't yet have to face his new owner's demands, he didn't dare indulge for long. His time was not his own to spend, after all, and his body not his own to please.

He toweled off and opened the bathroom door, realizing only then that his master hadn't left him any clothes to change into, or told him where to go when he was done. He was saved by an, "In here, Daniel," drifting in from the adjacent room—Carl's bedroom, he assumed.

Naked, then. Obviously the master wanted him that way.

Even though he'd been called, he knocked when he approached the open door, just to be safe. Carl waved him in.

The man was sitting up in bed against the headboard, fully—and blessedly—clothed. His appraising stare was back, a little more overtly hungry than last time, openly approving. Daniel felt himself flush, and again tried to stuff his hands into pockets that didn't exist.

"Come here, Daniel." Carl patted the bed.

Daniel approached slowly, trepidation in every step, trying desperately not to think about the last time he'd been bent naked over a piece of furniture. He stiffened when Carl grabbed his wrist and pulled him close, but dared offer no resistance as Carl studied his fingers, his palm, the slave cuff he wore.

"Stunning," Carl said, one blunt finger tracing lines across his wrist. Daniel couldn't tell if the man was referring to his hand or the bracelet until a grin spread across Carl's face and he said, "You know, I could buy another whole slave with the hardware you're wearing. Think NewWorld would miss them?"

Daniel hesitantly allowed himself to smile back. "I think they'd notice, Master."

"Hmm," Carl grunted again. He patted the bed beside him once more, and Daniel sat down on the edge, fiercely aware of the press of his master's hip against his own. "Hungry?" Carl asked.

"No, sir. Uh, Master." Daniel was far too stressed to eat. Too stressed even to remember the proper honorific, it seemed.

Carl shrugged. "Suit yourself. And help yourself, too, if you change your mind later. Don't mind the weirdness; I'm allergic to gluten, or in other words, anything with flavor or texture. I'm afraid you'll have to suffer along with me."

"That's . . . that's okay, Master," Daniel said, because if the worst of his suffering here ended up being gluten-free waffles, he might actually start believing in God again. And also because he had no idea how else to respond. Things were starting to feel a bit surreal. Why all the dancing around? Why wasn't Carl just taking what he'd paid for? Getting it over with and letting him sleep?

As if reading his thoughts, Carl said, "You must be tired."

He was. He hadn't slept well all week, and it was almost midnight now, and the car would be here in ten hours to pick him up. "Well, then." Carl shifted over to the other side of the bed and pulled Daniel into the space he'd just vacated. He kicked his pants off, but left on his boxers and undershirt, much to Daniel's confusion, and crawled under the covers. "Good night, Daniel," he said. "Jane will wake us in the morning."

Good night? Jane?

Really?

Carl snapped the light off, rolled away from Daniel, and promptly began to snore.

Oh, how Daniel envied him.

CHAPTER THREE

Daniel slept poorly. Many long minutes passed before he could even bring himself to lie down beside Carl, and many more still before the tension in his body began to uncoil, before he was able to convince himself nothing would happen tonight and he should really get some sleep lest he space out again at work. Which led, inevitably, to thoughts of the waiting discipline, which made sleep even *more* elusive. They'd have gotten it over with last night if not for this new arrangement, which he was starting to feel awfully bitter about again; if not for Carl, he wouldn't be lying here sleepless with nerves, wouldn't have to worry about making it through the broadcast tomorrow. Ten hours wasn't much time to get his shit together if they really hurt him. And they'd damn well expect him to smile for the camera when eight o'clock rolled around.

His stomach rumbled in the darkness, and he contemplated the freedom Carl had given him to help himself to food. But he didn't know how deep a sleeper the man was, and was frankly terrified of waking him. Better, he decided, to go hungry.

Finally, he closed his eyes and drifted into a fitful sleep.

He awoke in the morning in a minor panic, lying in an unfamiliar bed and staring at an unfamiliar ceiling. He couldn't remember where he was, which by itself was no big deal; he traveled often enough and on little enough sleep to be accustomed to waking disoriented. No, it was the arm draped over his naked waist and the large erection pressed up against his hip that was freaking him out. Instinct told him to bolt, but long, painful years of training told him to lie the fuck still and maybe, if he was lucky, successfully pretend he was still sleeping.

But then the hand tightened around his waist and the erection dug hard into his hip, and a deep voice rumbled, "Good morning," by his ear on a little puff of moist warmth.

Carl. New master.

Daniel stiffened, then forced himself to unstiffen lest Carl feel it. It wasn't good to show fear. People used fear against you.

"I know you're awake," Carl—*no, Master; don't forget again*—said, sleepy but in seemingly good humor.

"Yes, Master." Daniel opened his eyes, but didn't twitch a single muscle. He was afraid to find out what the master would do if he tried to sit up, pull away, what the master would do if he accidentally pressed back against that cock still digging into his hip.

But the master just flopped onto his back, scratched at his belly, and yawned. "Well," he said, tossing off the covers and lumbering to his feet. "I gotta piss. Breakfast's in . . ." He squinted at the clock until Daniel, still half-paralyzed with nerves and confusion but trained well enough to function beyond them, handed the man his glasses.

"Thank you," the master said, popping them on and yawning again. "In eighteen minutes. Go find Jane; she'll show you where your bathroom is. But I'm gonna shower, so don't run the hot water yet."

The master disappeared into the en suite before Daniel could reply or ask questions, like *Who's Jane?* or *What am I doing here?*

But he needed no answers to do as he'd been told, so with a pang of regret, he hauled himself out of bed. The mattress was much more luxurious than his own—some sort of memory foam, with a down comforter and what had to be at least thousand-count sheets. And he was so damn tired, not at all looking forward to his day. He was also buck naked, and didn't see any way to remedy that. Perhaps the master wanted him that way. He had no illusions about his body, or the way it made others react. Neither did NewWorld, who oversaw his diet and fitness regimen as strictly as they did his work schedule.

He heard the shower turn on, and, figuring he'd have at least a few minutes alone, permitted himself a moment of study. The bedroom was done up in shades of navy and beige, the furniture modern and sleek. His master had a scattering of photographs on the dresser, some framed football cards on the wall, an autographed ball on his desk. The room was so clean it practically sparkled, but Daniel was fairly certain that wasn't the master's doing. He obviously owned at least one more slave. Jane, presumably.

Great. How many people would see his pasty white ass this morning? Or maybe not so white—he was blushing full force when he stepped into the hall, where the smell of breakfast cooking hit him square in the nose. His stomach rumbled, but he was used to being hungry—had spent much of his childhood that way—and gave it no more thought.

When he came into the kitchen, he saw a pretty little white woman about his age, wearing jeans and a blouse and an apron covered in footballs, busy at the stove with what looked like eggs and (presumably gluten-free) pancakes. Lovely bracelets of spun gold sparkled on both her wrists.

"Jane?"

She turned and smiled at him, went back to the food for half a second, then whipped her head around again, her smile widening. "My my." She eyed him downright lewdly, but with a glimmer of amusement that smoothed Daniel's hackles. "This is more of you than I usually see on the evening news."

Daniel chuckled nervously and put the kitchen table between him and her. "Yeah, I uh, I don't know what happened to my clothes."

"You should forget them; think of the *ratings*."

Daniel bit his lip and ducked his head, and finally Jane took mercy on him. "Right there, darling," she said through a grin that looked ready to break with laughter. She pointed her spatula at a neatly folded pile on the far counter. Daniel nodded, but made no move to take them. "You can put them on, you know. Master never said a thing about you streaking through the apartment all morning."

"Uh, thanks."

"Our bathroom's just through there." She pointed with the spatula again to a hallway off the kitchen opposite the one that led to the master's room. "You have the red toothbrush. Don't know what kind of razor you like, but Dave's got an electric and a few different disposables, so take your pick. Breakfast in five, okay?"

Daniel nodded, wondering who Dave was and whether this morning could get any stranger. He somehow managed to brush his teeth and shave and get dressed in the time allotted. His clothes, apparently, had been laundered while he'd slept.

When he came back into the kitchen, a male slave was setting the table with two plates, two glasses, two sets of silverware. "Dave?" he guessed.

The man turned around and offered a smile and a handshake. "Yup."

Daniel hesitated, but he supposed this was a private place, and they could touch if the master allowed it—and presumably Dave wouldn't have offered if the master didn't. Dave's handshake was firm, and Daniel's eyes were drawn to the gold bracelets around his wrists, a more masculine version of the ones Jane wore. He was a handsome man, black hair buzzed short, eyes and skin such a rich dark shade of brown that his ancestors had likely never suffered a master's unwanted attention—a spectacular rarity after four centuries of opportunity to interbreed. He was bigger than Daniel by significant degrees—easily as tall as the master and twice as strong. The kind of man Daniel might go for if NewWorld didn't keep such a tight lock on that sort of behavior.

"Welcome to the family, Daniel. Please, sit." Dave pulled out a chair and gestured toward it. "The master wants you to eat with him this morning."

Daniel did as he was told, watching Dave and Jane and wondering if he looked anywhere near as lost as he felt. He probably did, because Dave clapped him on the shoulder and said, "Don't worry. Master Whitman's a good man. Just try to relax and be yourself." Then he turned to Jane, kissed her on the lips, and said, "I'll see you tonight, babe," before leaving the apartment for Daniel couldn't even imagine where.

"It's true," Jane said, sliding an omelet and a stack of pancakes onto each plate. "Master didn't have any use for Dave, but he bought him anyway, never mind he'd never owned even one slave before us, had no idea what was involved in taking care of us. Insisted he'd learn; didn't want to break up a couple, he said. Master rents Dave out now for construction work, but he's all mine in the evenings."

"And I just might make my money back before he's eighty," the master called from the entranceway. His hair was still damp, and he was suppressing a smile as he slid into the seat next to Daniel. "Morning, Jane."

She greeted him back and poured him a glass of juice, then disappeared.

The master attacked his breakfast, downing half his omelet without sparing Daniel a single glance. When at last he did look, he saw that Daniel hadn't yet touched his food and frowned. "What? You don't like eggs?"

"No, Master, I . . . I mean, of course I like eggs. It's just, you didn't—"

"*Oh*," the master said, theatrically loud, drawing out the single word into at least four syllables. "Right. NewWorld with all its *rules*. God, the stick up its ass must reach all the way to Australia." Daniel grimaced at the dig on his corporate master, at his new master so casually taking the Lord's name in vain like he didn't care who heard him. But the master didn't seem to notice, just kept on talking. "You're waiting for *permission*, aren't you?" Daniel nodded, and the master shrugged, waved at his plate. "Well, go on then. Eat." He took another bite of his own breakfast, then mumbled around a mouthful of pancake, "Everyone trains 'em different. I never know how to handle you people."

They spent the rest of the morning in a strange, semitense silence. Daniel was practically vibrating on the couch as the master, lounging in his recliner with the sports pages, wordlessly passed him sections of the *New York Times* and the *Washington Post*. Daniel had heard that companions knelt naked on the floor at their master's feet, but his master had asked no such thing of him. Hadn't even touched him, really, except this morning in his sleep. Maybe that wasn't his intent after all; maybe he really had bought him for something different: to discuss ideas, or talk about the news, or . . . Daniel chuffed quietly. *Yeah, right.*

Jane flitted in the background, dusting and straightening and washing. At 9:50 a.m., she leaned over Daniel's shoulder and whispered, "Your car will be here in ten minutes," then went back to her work. Daniel glanced up at the master, who was buried waist deep in little teepee'd stacks of newspaper sections, scribbling on a notepad, and cleared his throat. He didn't dare leave without approval, no matter how permissive the master had been so far—or how derisive he'd been of NewWorld's training—but he also didn't dare speak out of turn.

His master either didn't hear him or chose to ignore him, so he tried again, a little more deliberately this time. The master flipped the page with a loud rustle and a sigh and said, "*Yes*, Daniel? What is it? Speak."

"I, uh, it's almost ten, Master."

"Yes, yes." Carl shooed him away without even glancing up from his paper. "Go. I'll see you tonight."

CHAPTER FOUR

The moment Daniel stepped onto the news floor, he began to think he'd rather have stayed in his new master's awkward company. A grim-faced Tim cut him off halfway to his office.

"Don't even bother," Tim said, steering him away from the office and back toward the hallway. "They're pissed. Don't be late."

Daniel's feet froze up for a second, and Tim gave his arm a harsh jerk, pulling him along. "You said you'd be good," Tim snapped, then, "Sorry, sorry," when Daniel let his hurt show on his face. "It's just, like I said, they're pissed, and I worry about you."

"I know."

"Look . . ." Tim pushed the elevator call button and waited for the car to arrive. "Do you want me to—?"

"No." Bad enough Tim would see the aftermath; Daniel didn't want to put him through the main event.

"I can come down there after, if you want. Come and get you."

The elevator dinged, and Daniel stepped inside. "I'm a big boy, Tim. I'll be fine."

Tim didn't look convinced, but then the elevator door closed, and what Tim thought ceased to matter.

At 10:27 a.m., Daniel found himself in a plain little room in the basement of NewWorld Media's US headquarters, empty but for leather shackles bolted to the top and bottom of a pole near one wall, and four chairs lined up against the opposite wall. Soundproof paneling lined every surface. After all, it wouldn't do to upset the freemen upstairs with all that unseemly screaming.

Three of the four chairs were occupied. Daniel was an important slave, so he was dismayed—but not surprised—to see some important people. Ben Cheng, Chief of US Programming, looking sad, angry, and disappointed all at once; Eric Foster, the HR boss who'd replaced Daniel's savior over a decade ago; and his own chief executive producer, Maxwell Epstein, looking about as unhappy as Ben. The fourth seat was reserved for Daniel's handler, but Tim wasn't obliged to watch, and Daniel was grateful he wasn't here.

Daniel stripped off his clothes without a word and knelt at their feet, head bowed.

"Do you know what you've done wrong, Daniel?" Ben asked.

"Yes, sir."

"Look at me."

Daniel took a deep breath and dragged his gaze up from the floor to Ben's stern face.

"Tell me." Ben's tone was no more yielding than his expression.

"I, uh . . ." Daniel swallowed hard, and his eyes drifted to the heavy leather strap on Mr. Foster's lap, then back to Ben. "I let myself get distracted. I was late to call yesterday. I missed my cue to open the show. I stumbled pretty badly a few times. And I might have zoned a little during the panel talk in C block."

"A *little*?" Maxwell said.

"And it wasn't just yesterday, was it?" Ben said. "All week you've been doing this. What's gotten into you?"

"I—"

"Haven't we been good to you?" Mr. Foster asked.

"Of course, sir! I just . . ." Daniel swallowed again, shook his head. "I'm sorry, sirs. I won't try to make excuses." His gaze was drawn to the strap again, and he added softly, "And I won't struggle. I promise."

"Wow. Good for you," Mr. Foster sneered. "You don't get a medal for taking what's coming to you like a properly trained slave, you know."

"I know, sir, I didn't mean it like that, I—"

Maxwell held out a hand, silencing Daniel *and* Mr. Foster, who'd clearly been winding up to shout again. Daniel dared to hope for leniency for just a fraction of a second, but then the pity on Maxwell's face was overshadowed by grim disappointment, and he shook his head and said, "I'm afraid that's not good enough this time, Daniel."

Daniel's head snapped up even as his gut sank like a concrete block in the East River. "Sir?"

"Four years ago, we took a *huge* risk on you, Daniel."

"I know, sir, and I'm forever grateful."

"Giving a slave his own show. You know how often that happens, Daniel?" He didn't beyond *hardly never*, but it didn't matter; the question was clearly rhetorical. "And when we did that, you swore to us that you would treat it as the solemn responsibility it was. You swore to us that nothing, *nothing* would ever interfere with you putting on the best damn newscast on television."

Daniel nodded. He *had* said that, and he knew damn well he'd made a liar of himself this week. Let his supervisors down. And let his brethren down too, because who here would ever again trust another slave with that kind of responsibility if even their star pupil couldn't hack it?

"I need you back on your game, Daniel. All of us have superiors to answer to, not to mention investors, you understand me?"

"Yes, sir." *Not just my ass on the line. Check.*

"So tell me we're not going to discipline you now and just have to drag you back here tomorrow."

"We know you were nervous about the leasing program," Mr. Foster chimed in before Daniel could reply. "But the anticipation's over now, right? Your first night's done, you're here, you're fine, your world is still in one piece, yes?"

"Yes, sir," Daniel agreed, but in truth he wasn't so sure.

"The leasing program is just as important to the company right now as your show is," Mr. Cheng said. "Do you understand?"

"Yes, sir."

"Do you know how much of our revenue this year will come from the leases?" When Daniel shook his head, Mr. Cheng said, "Six percent, Daniel. *Six percent.*"

"Look." Mr. Foster again. "Maybe we've spoiled you. Maybe we've been too soft. Or maybe you've just forgotten what you are. I can't imagine why else you'd think it acceptable to sulk and stumble your way through an entire week of work over this. But you need to get your shit together, Daniel. We need you present and focused in that newsroom, and we need you gracious and obedient in your master's home. If he so much as *thinks* a single upsetting thought about you, you're going to end up right back in here, you understand?"

"Yes, sir," Daniel said, but the tremble in his voice gave him away. He and Carl hadn't exactly seemed to hit it off.

"I mean it, Daniel. Don't make the mistake of thinking you're special, or worse, irreplaceable. Don't think that being on camera will protect you."

"I don't, sir."

Except he sort of had, hadn't he? He'd even said as much when Carl had asked him what they'd do to him—*I need to be able to sit through the broadcast*, he'd said. So blithely assumed. That concrete block churned in his gut as he realized how wrong he'd been.

Stupid slave cunt.

"Get up."

Daniel flinched a little at the tone but did as he was told, trying to hold himself tall as he approached the pole. He fisted it tightly in both hands, but Mr. Foster said, "No," and pulled Daniel's hands away to buckle them into the restraints.

Daniel didn't fight him, but his arms started shaking hard enough to make Mr. Foster's task a challenge. He couldn't help it; he looked back over his shoulder at Maxwell—his EP, his guardian and champion and protector for the last four years—and let his eyes plead for answers to questions he didn't dare voice.

Maxwell grimaced and snapped, "For God's sake, Eric, *talk* to him. Can't you see he's scared?"

Mr. Foster gave Daniel's left wrist a hard tug to check the buckle and then started strapping in the right one. "I know you *think* you'll hold still," he said, "but we have a point to drive home today, and we're going to make damn well sure you learn your lesson."

That was supposed to be *comforting*? Daniel couldn't stop himself this time; he stuttered, "H-How . . . how many?"

"Seventy."

"*What?*" Daniel blurted, breathy and astonished, and holy shit had he just questioned his betters in that tone of voice? He'd be lucky if they didn't *kill* him.

Mr. Foster dug his nails into Daniel's bare shoulder and shook him. "Ten for each day this week you dropped the ball, ten for being late to call, ten for missing your cue, ten for fumbling the panel."

He realized he'd begun to struggle against the restraints and forced himself still, but his eyes, no doubt revealing the depths of his panic, once again sought reassurance from Maxwell.

This time, though, Maxwell shook his head. "We're all in agreement, Daniel. I'm sorry."

"Please don't do this," Daniel whispered.

"Daniel—"

"But I have to go on air toni—"

"Stop talking, Daniel," Maxwell said, calm but unarguable, at the same time Mr. Foster said, "See, this is exactly what we're talking about. You *have* forgotten your place."

Then he stepped back, grabbed the strap, and struck him.

The first blow landed high across the shoulders, hard enough to knock him off-balance, but more heat and sound than pain. The heat became a burn at the second blow, and all-out fire at the third. The fourth was agony; he didn't bother trying to stay quiet.

Mr. Foster laid orderly stripes, working down from Daniel's shoulders. By the time the strap reached the small of his back, the whole of his existence had been swallowed by a single, blazing supernova of heat and pain, ebbing slightly through each short pause and swelling tenfold when the next strike hit.

When the strap carved a line into the upper curve of his ass, he couldn't even hear Mr. Foster counting anymore over the rushing in his ears and the sound of his own cries.

A new ebb, long enough for him to settle, to stop screaming for a moment. Seventy was a *lot*; Mr. Foster's arm was probably tired. Maybe he was taking a break.

Or maybe not. Daniel felt the whisper of air before the next blow landed like a strip of razor wire across his ass, heard Mr. Foster say, "Fifty-three," and buried his face in his arm to hold back a sob.

Agony in his shoulders, his back, his ass, bleeding into his thighs and calves. He didn't remember them chaining his ankles, but obviously they had because he couldn't get away, couldn't escape it, though he struggled and fought and begged and made promises he knew he couldn't keep.

Then the noise fell away, and the flame slowly cooled from white to blue to red, and he heard someone say, ". . . now, Daniel. Easy, buddy. Easy."

Slowly, slowly, reality began to creep back into his awareness—the cold pole, the white walls, his harsh, ragged breathing, a roiling nausea creeping up his throat, and pain, *God . . .* The pain was so bad he couldn't think beyond it, didn't even realize for several moments that the beating had stopped and he was slumped against the pole, dangling by his wrists, tears leaking from his eyes. "'m I . . ." He panted, wanting to ask if it was over but unable to convince his lips and tongue to function.

There was a bottle of water at his mouth then, and a gentle hand in his sweat-soaked hair, and he swished and spat and took a long swallow, but that little bit of moisture had no hope at all of dousing the flames still curling straight through to his bones.

"Can you stand?"

He heard but couldn't quite process the question. Felt the pull in his shoulders and elbows and wrists but couldn't figure out how to make it stop. Just hung there, chest heaving, chasing oxygen from the superheated air, cheek pressed to the cool metal of the pole.

More words bled through his haze, and then there were hands on his wrists and ankles undoing his bonds, a shoulder under his arm to stop him from falling. He turned slowly and blinked up at Maxwell, lifted a numb, trembling hand to wipe tears from his face. "'s done?" he asked.

Maxwell eased him to the floor and propped him against his chest, saying, "Yeah. All done."

Daniel closed his eyes and let his head fall against Maxwell's shoulder, struggling to rein in his frantic breaths, to push the agony back far enough to function through. His fingers clenched tight in Maxwell's shirt, and he mumbled, "'m sorry," then said it again, a little stronger, just to make sure he'd been heard.

"I know," Maxwell said, his hand smoothing across Daniel's hair.

"'m I bleeding?"

"A little. Just a few shallow cuts; some Band-Aids will do the trick."

That was hard to believe given the way he felt, but Daniel knew his boss wouldn't lie to him. He was still panting into Maxwell's shoulder, fighting to pull himself together, when Maxwell asked, "You going to be sick?"

Unable to speak anymore, Daniel just shook his head. He heard someone say, "Better go get Tim," and then nothing else for a while.

CHAPTER FIVE

Daniel woke up facedown on the couch in his office, pulled from sleep by an insistent, throbbing burn from his calves to his shoulders. He made the mistake of trying to sit up and groaned, fisting hands into the cushions and panting until the spots faded from his eyes.

"Here." A hand holding three Tylenol and a bottle of water moved into his peripheral vision. He had to sit up to swallow the pills, and the hand helped him with that too. The world grayed out for a second, and when it came back, he was leaning shoulder to shoulder with Tim, carefully keeping the pressure off most of the welts on his back.

"Fuck," he said softly after swallowing the pills.

"Yeah," Tim agreed.

Daniel took a long pull on his water and asked, a hint of accusation in his tone, "Did you know it was going to be that bad?"

Tim shook his head, a silent apology stamped on his face that they both knew Daniel didn't deserve.

"Did I— I think I fought them."

"A little toward the end there, Maxwell said. You must've been out of your head by then, though. Nobody blames you." Tim smiled wanly and added, "That's why God made restraints, right?"

Another swig, and the bottle was empty. Tim magically produced a new one, and Daniel chugged half of that down, too. He felt like he'd sweated out gallons of water. "How'd I get here?"

"Walked. I came and got you. Don't you remember?"

He closed his eyes, probed gently backward. His postpunishment memories were empty of all but agony and a vague recollection of Maxwell stroking his hair. "How long was I out?"

"About half an hour. And I'm afraid I have more bad news for you."

Eyes still closed, Daniel dropped his aching head in his hands and moaned.

"You haven't done anything wrong," Tim said, patting his knee. "Well, nothing *new* wrong. But given your recent lapses and the identity of your new master, corporate has asked me to talk to you about confidentiality."

Daniel was too pissy and in too much pain to censor himself in front of Tim; he side-eyed the guy with real malice and spat, "Oh, what, you think I'm going to spill company secrets to Carl while he's got his cock shoved up my ass?"

Tim winced. *Good.* Daniel was equally glad—though not at all surprised—to see no anger at all on Tim's face. Just guilt and sympathy. "Come on, Daniel, that's not fair. You know I trust you. It's just . . . there's always a potential for corporate espionage, and your master's a clever man, and he's in a position of power over you. Nonetheless, you still have an obligation to protect the intellectual property of this company and its standing in the rankings."

Daniel's expression didn't change at all; he felt ugly, accusing, the anger in him rising by the second. "You're right. He *is* in a position of power over me. In case you couldn't tell from all the welts on my back, I'm not exactly allowed to tell him no. What am I supposed to say if he asks, huh?" He wanted to stand, to stare Tim down, to shake him until he admitted how unfair the world was. But he did none of those things, couldn't trust even Tim's goodwill that far. Said instead, soft and wounded, "How could you put me in this position?"

Tim's gaze slunk away from Daniel's, and even through the fury, the betrayal, Daniel felt a little thrill of satisfaction at that, at the tacit acknowledgment. "Carl knows the rules, Daniel. He knows you're not allowed to discuss confidential information, and if he tries to punish you for upholding your duties to this company, he'll lose his leasing rights *and* the money he paid for them." Tim paused a moment, like he was hoping Daniel would say, *Oh, okay, that makes everything just peachy, then.* When Daniel didn't, Tim added, gaze still on the floor, "So, look, I know it can be a sticky situation, and I'm sorry about that, but you'll just have to work around it if it comes up."

Great. Just fucking *great.* An hour ago, he'd been terrified that Carl had only leased him to fuck him. Now he was terrified that Carl had leased him to talk to him, and he'd slip up and say something he shouldn't have and he'd end up right back in the basement, or worse.

Tim patted his knee again. Stood. "I promise it's not as dire as it sounds, Daniel. You'll be fine. Just … no discussing active investigations or rankings or ad strategies, okay?"

Daniel nodded, because what else was he supposed to do but agree, and also because maybe, just maybe, Tim was right. NewWorld had always taken care of him before, hadn't they? Surely they wouldn't endanger him now. Besides, he was just as clever as Carl was. He'd find a way to make it work. NewWorld *trusted* him to find a way to make it work.

"It's time to get back to work now, I'm afraid."

Of course it was. He'd lost half the morning already to his own bad behaviors and fears. "Can I do it from the couch?"

"Sure. I'll go get your laptop."

Daniel spent his afternoon working on his belly, his entire back side covered with chemical ice packs courtesy of Tim. Focus shot, he accomplished little, but he trusted in his staff to pick up the slack. Though he didn't remember it happening, they all must have seen him stumbling back from the elevator, clinging to Tim, tears staining his face; he knew most of them would put their hearts into making his life a little easier this afternoon. Maxwell never hired anyone who had issues "working for" a slave, and certainly plenty enough of them were slaves themselves, well familiar with the pain of a hard strapping. Tim wasn't pushing him at all, and even Maxwell admitted that after so severe a punishment, he'd expected to have to call in a sub for tonight's broadcast. Daniel was adamant that he could do it himself, though. He didn't think Mr. Foster would be as understanding as Maxwell, and it wasn't like he'd get to go home to his little cubbyhole anyway.

Really, all he wanted to do was crawl off and be alone, lick his wounds in private, but he had a new master now, and what he wanted had never mattered very much anyway. He shuddered at the thought of his master making him strip again, studying him like a fucking bug, pressing fingers into his welts and bruises and getting off on his pain.

Maybe, he told himself, it wouldn't be so bad. Maybe the master really wasn't a sick fuck. Maybe he'd even ignore Daniel.

Sure, yeah. And maybe Daniel would sprout wings and fly to freedom in Scandinavia. Because the only other way he was getting out of his obligations was in a fucking wooden box.

Tim returned a few hours later with three more Tylenol, two fresh ice packs, and a sandwich that was most definitely not from the slaves' cafeteria.

"Thank you," Daniel said, swallowing the pills and sitting on the ice packs, but eying the sandwich warily. He was still hurting just enough to be queasy and didn't much feel like puking.

"Nonoptional," Tim said, plunking it in his lap. "Eat. You missed lunch, and the pills will upset your stomach if it's empty. On a different note, there's a production meeting in twenty minutes—think you can make it?"

Daniel took a bite of sandwich—BLT on whole wheat, just how he liked it: lightly toasted, no mayo, extra tomato—and shrugged. It was a stupid thing to do; abused nerves fired from his shoulder to his tailbone, and he hissed, swallowed a piece of bacon the wrong way and spent the next thirty seconds trying to cough up the food and half his lung.

"Just not your day, is it?" Tim said when Daniel could breathe again, half teasing, half deadly serious. He hovered close, but when it was clear that Daniel was done coughing, he pointed a finger at the sandwich, said, "Eat," one more time, and left Daniel's office, closing the door behind him.

Blissfully alone, if only for the moment, Daniel did as he was told. Surprisingly, he felt a bit better after eating. He even managed to drag his sorry ass to the production meeting, and while it wasn't one of his shining moments, at least he got through it. When he fell asleep for an hour on his couch afterward, nobody seemed to notice. If they did, they held their tongues.

Tim returned again at seven with more food, a Percocet, and a large espresso. Daniel raised his eyebrows at the combination.

"The consensus is that a sleepy you is better than a sweating you," Tim said. "This ought to let you grit through the broadcast without drooping too much."

"Thanks," Daniel said, and not just to be polite. It wasn't often that a slave got nursed through discipline on painkillers of any sort, let alone narcotics. He didn't like espresso, but he knew the drugs would knock him cold without the caffeine, so he took a sip anyway.

"And I gotta tell ya, this whole waiting hand and foot on a slave thing is mighty inconvenient. So next time you're thinking about doing something stupid and getting your ass beat, could you maybe, you know, *not*? Or at least do it on a Friday?"

The apology was already passing through Daniel's lips when he glanced up and saw Tim's smile. He smiled back, touched his fingers to Tim's arm, and looked him straight in the eye. "Really, Tim, I mean it. Thanks."

The broadcast was its own special level of Hell, but they'd arranged the night's rundown without panels or long interviews, minimizing his camera time. He stood through all the pretaped packages and sat on ice packs during the intros and extros, careful not to lean back against his chair. His skin still felt too tight, terribly oversensitized, burning like he'd been dipped in menthol, and he'd been unable to suppress more than one wince when he'd moved a little too much or too fast. But at least the pain kept him alert, actually helped him to focus—if for no other reason than it served as a constant reminder of what would happen if he screwed up again.

They let him go at 9:05, after taping a quick look-live for the morning. Tim was waiting for him in his office, and Daniel's heart double-timed it when he saw him. Had he done something wrong again?

"Easy," Tim said, as if reading his mind, or perhaps just the fear on his face. "You were fine. I just came to give you this for the road." Another Percocet was sitting in Tim's upturned hand. "Our secret, okay?"

Daniel took it with a weary nod, stuck it in his pocket. The two of them stood silently then, Tim focused on Daniel, Daniel too tired to focus on much of anything at all.

"You should change," Tim finally said. "You're on borrowed time now, remember?"

Daniel nodded, started fumbling at his tie with clumsy fingers. After a few failed attempts at loosening the knot, Tim nudged Daniel's hands away and untied it for him.

"I can't wear the suit out just this once?" Daniel asked. Just the *thought* of pulling his formfitting jeans over the welts on his calves, thighs, and ass made him grimace.

Tim shook his head. "You know the rules, Daniel. Come on, I'll help you."

Tim started making work of the buttons on Daniel's shirt, and with a heavy sigh, Daniel pulled the pill from his pocket and swallowed it dry.

CHAPTER SIX

Daniel fell asleep on the short ride to his master's, sprawled on his belly across the back seat of the sedan. He awoke with a gasp when the doorman opened the door and gave his shoulder a shake. The man snatched his hand back with a hasty apology, but then leaned in again, helping to extricate a sweating, swearing Daniel from the car.

"Didn't think they did this to guys like you," the doorman said as he walked Daniel to the elevator, and it was all Daniel could do not to snap back, *What the fuck does* that *mean?* Guys like *him?* He was a slave, just like the doorman. Just a damn slave.

And he was reminded quite firmly of that when his master led him to the center of the living room without so much as a greeting and said, "Strip."

It must have taken him five minutes to wriggle out of his clothes, but his master didn't seem to be in any particular hurry. He was lounging on the couch, arms stretched across the back cushions, the ankle of one leg resting on the opposite knee. His eyes were intent on Daniel, but his face was completely neutral. What was he thinking? Was he enjoying this? What did he *want?*

Daniel peeled off his left sock and placed it neatly atop the rest of his clothes on the couch. Naked at last, he stood as straight as he could manage, feeling flush and fighting back a yawn and the urge to fidget.

"Turn around," the master said, his voice more soft and even than seemed possible from such a large man.

Normally, Daniel would have been relieved to obey, to hide his nudity, but today presented a whole new world of vulnerabilities. He'd caught a glimpse of himself in the mirror in his office as Tim had helped him change, seen the head-to-toe bruising, the red welts that stood out bright against pale skin, the dozen or so cuts across his right shoulder blade and hip where the tip of the strap had landed too hard too close to bone. There was an intimacy to letting someone see those things that went beyond nudity: a weakness, a failure, a helplessness painted on his skin for this stranger to see. To jack off to, even, for all he fucking knew.

But who was he kidding; he wasn't *letting*. There were no choices here. Not for him. NewWorld had driven that home rather agonizingly hard today.

He turned around.

Silence, save a rustling behind him, a single footstep on the carpeted floor, and then curious fingers traced blazing paths down his back that made him gasp and flinch.

Please don't hurt me anymore, he prayed. *I can't, I'm done, it's too much*, and like some miracle from the God he no longer believed in, the fingers disappeared. And then so did his master, leaving him alone in the middle of the living room, wondering what the hell he was supposed to do now.

The master came back a minute later with a yawning Jane trailing behind, dressed in pajamas, hair tousled. She took one look at Daniel hunched and shivering by the coffee table and said, "Oh, *darling*."

"Fix him, would you?" the master said, casually gruff, as if he'd handed her a shirt to mend or a broken heel to repair, and then ambled off to his bedroom.

What? What was *happening* here?

Jane touched a hand to Daniel's arm and gently turned him to face her. It was strange how unself-conscious he suddenly felt; maybe he was just too weary to be bothered with such things, or maybe too confused. Jane was looking at him like his mother used to after his old mistress got a hold of him, and it made him warm in a way that had nothing to do with pain or shame.

"Sorry to wake you," he mumbled as she led him the two steps to the couch, laid him down on his belly like he was made of glass, and ran a hand across his hair.

"Don't be silly," she chided. "You just rest. I'll be right back."

She returned with cool washcloths and hydrogen peroxide and a cold, sweet-smelling cream that numbed his skin as she rubbed it into his legs and back. "Was this because of yesterday?" she asked as she worked. Daniel nodded, too tired to clarify, already feeling better than he had all day. "I saw you tonight, knew what happened right away. Don't tell him I told you, but the master looked quite upset."

He did? Daniel wanted to press her about that, but said instead, "I thought I was careful."

Jane smeared some cream into his shoulder. "I don't think most people noticed. Master just knew what to look for."

"And you?"

Her hand froze momentarily on his shoulder blade. She didn't reply, but Daniel could read the truth in her face—a dark history there to match his own—and he let it go.

"All right, darling," she said, clearing her throat and wiping her hands on a washcloth, "that's as good as I can make it. Off you go now. Master's waiting."

Daniel paced toward the master's bedroom, telling himself over and over that he could sleep soon, that in a few moments this day would be over and he could close his eyes and put it all behind him.

The alternatives did not bear considering.

Still uncertain of the rules, he knocked on the open door. His master, propped against the headboard, looked up from his book— *The Slavery Fallacy* by Nathaniel Bishops, Daniel was surprised to note; Carl didn't strike him as a typical consumer of ultra-left-wing rhetoric, especially from an atheist British barrister—and patted the empty space beside him. When Daniel hesitated at the bedside, not wanting to smear cream on the sheets (never mind how much sitting would hurt), his master said, "It's okay. You can lie down if you want to."

He wanted to very much, so he eased onto his belly, tucking his arms beneath the pillow, facing his master's hip. His eyes drifted closed, but the sound of a flipping page pulled him from the beginnings of sleep. A moment later, he felt a hand on his head, heavy and warm, still but for two fingers making short, tentative strokes through the hair at his nape.

He stiffened and squeezed his eyes closed, focusing on controlling his breathing. What was *wrong* with him? When Jane had done the same thing just minutes before, he'd taken pleasure from her touch. Why did the same touch frighten him so much when the hand belonged to his master?

Because he can hurt you.

Not to mention the issue of Daniel's desires, for as much as they ever mattered for anything. And maybe choice as well; Jane didn't expect compliance or false affection from him. He could tell her no.

The hand disappeared just long enough to flip another page, then returned again, bolder this time. Fingers traced the shell of his ear, the line of his jaw. A thumb brushed across his lips, pushing a little; Daniel unclenched his jaw just enough to allow the thumb the entrance it demanded. It explored the inside of his lower lip, touched his teeth, then pulled away to turn another page.

Daniel fisted both hands in his pillow and prayed those fingers would stay gone. He was breathing like he'd run a race, achingly tired but losing his grip on sleep so thoroughly that he feared he might not reclaim it at all tonight.

The master's hand came back, and Daniel bit his tongue to keep in a whimper. For one horrifying moment, he thought he might cry. All he wanted to do was sleep, go back to his cubbyhole on the West Side and—

The hand stroked across his hip and derailed his train of thought. Probably for the best, anyway; wishing on things you could never have brought nothing but trouble. He held his breath, dreading where the exploring fingers might go next. When they skimmed featherlight down his welted ass, he couldn't help it—that damn whimper escaped his throat.

The master's hand froze, lifted away. "Did I hurt you?" he asked in that same soft, even tone from before.

A pause, and then, "Yes, Master." That was technically true, but in the larger scope of things, the pain had been nothing, and certainly not the real cause of his distress.

Still, this time when the hand disappeared, it didn't come back.

CHAPTER SEVEN

When Daniel awoke in the morning, the sun was already high in the sky, and Jane was standing over him, smiling bright.

"Good morning, darling."

"Mmph," was about all Daniel could think to reply. He felt logy, drugged, pain thrumming deep and hot enough to discourage full consciousness.

"Come on, then. Breakfast's waiting. Your car'll be here in forty-five minutes."

"*What*?" Daniel pushed up in a panic, grunted, and fell back to the bed. He realized the other side was empty; his master was gone. "It's *9:15*?"

"Master left early today. He thought you could use the sleep."

"Oh." Daniel blinked, sat up more carefully this time. It wasn't *too* bad—not nearly as bad as last night, at least—and he actually felt rested. Plus, he hadn't woken to a cock digging into his hip. Maybe things were looking up.

"Here." Jane stuffed a bundle of clothes into his hands once he was vertical. He shook it out to reveal a pair of navy track pants with a white stripe down each leg. They were new; the tag was still on.

"What's this?"

"Gift from the master. He thought your jeans would hurt."

"Oh," Daniel said again, rather stupidly, he thought. "That was . . . Really?"

Jane nodded, grinning wide, clearly as proud of the man as if she owned him and not the other way around.

"Wow, I've never . . . I mean, we're not allowed to own things at NewWorld. Causes fights, they say."

"Well then, you just bring them back tonight, is all." She plucked the pants from his slack fingers and folded them on the dresser, then pulled the little jar of numbing cream from her apron pocket. "Now lie back down, and I'll fix you up, and we'll get you on your way."

Breakfast was fresh fruit salad and some sort of home-baked, rice-flour blueberry muffins he felt certain he could eat for the rest of his life and never grow tired of. Jane hustled him through his new morning routine and deposited him in the waiting car herself at three minutes to ten. "Be good," she said as she closed the door, but what Daniel really heard was, "Be careful," or maybe, "Stay safe."

The day was long. Tim hovered, bringing him food and Tylenol and making excuses to check in, and Maxwell watched him closely enough to make him nervous. He'd lost almost two hours this morning oversleeping—time normally spent reading the day's papers—but worked furiously to catch up, taking the lead at the afternoon production meeting and hitting the show out of the park. It was easier to bury himself in work than to think about that finger on his lips, that hand on his ass. It was easier than thinking about the track pants he changed into to go home—or, at least, what passed for home now. He missed his cubbyhole. He missed his friends back in the dorm. He missed playing chess and listening in on sports conversations he knew nothing about and stealing quick, rough, fear-laced handjobs in the bathroom with that hot black line producer while supervisors with shock prods tucked into their belts prowled the floor.

If not for Carl, he would have slept in tomorrow, gotten up at ten or eleven, jogged the circuit in Central Park with Tim, then maybe read the new issue of the *Economist* and watched old movies in the little lounge at the end of his hall. He would have eaten dinner in the mess with his friends and had those cookies for dessert that the slave bakers in the InfoGlobe café always snuck back for their floors. And then, if he were *really* lucky, he'd have found an excuse—meeting a contact, or doing background research, perhaps—to lounge in the stacks at the Barnes & Noble or maybe see some live music in one of the few West Side clubs that permitted entrance to unattended slaves.

Instead, he'd be spending his weekend doing . . . well, he wasn't sure what, exactly, but he doubted he'd get to keep his new track pants on.

"Daniel?"

Tim. Daniel dropped the dress shirt he'd been holding and turned his gaze from the city lights out his office window to his handler.

"It's almost ten."

Shit, he'd been daydreaming for a long time.

"You have to go." Tim touched a hand to his back—*ow, fuck, not cool, Tim*—and guided him away from the view of Central Park, shrouded in what passed for darkness in this city. "You should have left half an hour ago."

"Sorry," he mumbled, scraping his teeth over his lower lip and staring at his sneakered feet as they carried him from his office.

"Please don't make me come in here again on Monday."

Tim's voice was soft, but the warning was clear, so Daniel said, "I won't."

Tim sighed and drew Daniel to a stop in the near-empty newsroom, looked him in the eye. For a moment, Daniel thought he might scold him, but instead he just shook his head and said, "I'm sorry you're unhappy."

Daniel waited for the rest—*But buck up, do your duty, your happiness has no bearing here*—but Tim just said good-night and sent him on his way.

CHAPTER EIGHT

The doorman told Daniel the penthouse was unlocked and to let himself in. Daniel was perfectly happy not to be led off the elevator by his master, but once he was standing in the condo, he had no idea what to do. He had no place here yet, no rules or boundaries. He didn't know what was okay to touch, or if he was allowed to sit, or if the offer to use the kitchen still stood. He wanted to shower, wash the makeup off his face, let the heat unclench the muscles in his back, but he didn't know if that was allowed either.

At a loss, Daniel tiptoed toward the slave suite. The light was on in the bathroom, but not the bedroom, and he could hear Dave snoring softly through the cracked-open door. There were lights on in the large, open kitchen/living room, but none down the hallway toward the guest room or his master's bedroom. Everyone was asleep.

He eyed the kitchen table and counters, the coffee table in the living room, looking for a note or directions or . . . *something*, his jaw cracking with a yawn as he walked a circuit around the room. He found nothing, but then, he hadn't expected to. His master had obviously assumed that Daniel would know what to do. Maybe, in his belligerence or his pain, he'd simply not heard whatever instructions his master had given. Or maybe Tim had told him, and he hadn't paid attention. He knew companions warmed their masters' beds, but was that . . . was he . . . ?

What if he accidentally woke the master? What if he went in there and his master didn't want him? The man would be angry; he would punish him. He would tell Mr. Foster.

Better not risk it. He'd sleep on the couch.

Except, he didn't know if he was allowed to do *that*, either. His first mistress *never* let him on the furniture.

Fuck it. He'd sleep on the floor.

Thank God for carpeting. The floor was hard and chilly, but at least not unbearably so. He fell asleep on his belly but woke up sometime in the middle of the night, curled on his side, shivering cold and with a crick in his neck. Misery prompted a moment's contemplation of crawling into his master's warm bed, but in the end, he simply pulled his arms into the sleeves of his T-shirt and propped a sneaker under his head in lieu of a pillow.

When next he awoke, it was morning, and his pajama-clad master was standing over him, arms crossed, hair rumpled, looking decidedly unhappy.

"I woke up and my bed was cold," the master snapped.

Daniel popped his arms from his sleeves and bolted to his knees, barely feeling the pain or stiffness in his body over the sudden panic and the rabbitlike thumping of his heart. "I'm sorry, Master," he blurted, because the master was *pissed* and he was going to tell Mr. Foster and Daniel could barely *breathe*. He couldn't handle another trip down to the basement, he *couldn't*. "I came home and everyone was sleeping and I didn't know what to—"

The master cut him off with an uncoordinated wave, then rubbed one eye with the hand he'd just flopped at Daniel. "I need caffeine before I can listen to this." *Cram the excuses, you dumb slave cunt. I'm not interested.* "What time is it? *Jane!*" Daniel flinched at the shouting; it took him a moment to realize it wasn't aimed at him. The master squinted at the kitchen, back at Daniel. "Where's Jane?"

"I, I don't—"

"No," the master sighed, this time rubbing his other eye. "Of course you don't. You just woke up too."

"I'm sor—"

"Yes yes, you're sorry, I get it, now please stop apologizing; it's fine."

It's . . . *what*? Daniel sucked in the deepest breath he could, tried to force his brain to *think*. Something was definitely not adding up here, and he was starting to get the sense that maybe this situation didn't actually call for panic.

The master turned his squint on Daniel. "Are you cold? You're shaking."

"Y-yes, Master, the floor is—"

He was cut off this time by Jane bustling through the front door with a brown paper bag tucked under one arm and a large steaming takeout cup in the other. She paused in the entranceway when she saw them, eyeing them both, but then stepped forward and held out the cup. "You're up early, Master. Grande soy latte, extra sugar."

The master snatched the cup from her hand and took a long swig. "Yeah, well, I woke up *alone* and got worried."

Daniel flinched again, but Jane just winked. "And grumpy, too." For *real*? Had she seriously just spoken to her master like that? "But cheer up, Master—the bakery had those gluten-free bagels you love. Still hot and everything."

The master grunted, but fell in line behind Jane, following her to the kitchen table and plopping down in a chair. She smeared some jelly on a bagel and gave it to him, then handed him two morning papers.

The master took a bite of his bagel, grunted in what appeared to be satisfaction, and flipped to the sports section of the *Times*. He looked pretty engrossed. Daniel considered getting off his knees, but he wasn't sure the master was done with him yet, and if the man had forgotten about him, he didn't want to do anything to redraw his attention.

Another bite, another little grunt-hum. Then the master put his bagel back on his plate, dropped the paper, and turned Daniel's way.

Daniel braced himself for whatever the master was about to demand or say.

But he just raised his eyebrows and asked, "Well? Do you want breakfast or not?"

For a moment, Daniel stared at him, speechless, until he remembered he was making eye contact with a freeman and dropped his chin. He'd screwed up, and the man wanted to *feed* him? Not exactly the reaction he'd been expecting, but he got himself together enough to nod, stutter out, "Y-yes, Master, thank you," and drag himself to his feet. God, he was *sore*. Sleeping on the floor sure hadn't helped.

The master tracked him as he walked around the couch and the counter that divided the kitchen from the living room. When Daniel reached the table, the master nudged the chair catty-corner to his with his foot. Daniel wasn't accustomed to eating with his betters, let alone right next to them; he hesitated, wincing as a spark of pain flared from his tailbone to his neck.

"Wait," the master said before Daniel could sit.

Shit. Had he blown it by hesitating? The master stood up from the table, and Daniel clenched his jaw, waiting for the blow, but the man stepped right past him and snatched a throw pillow from the couch, then placed it on Daniel's chair. "There," he said, waving once toward the chair before turning his attention back to his bagel and his paper.

Daniel eyed him, then the chair (which looked significantly more comfortable to his black-and-blue ass than it had just moments ago), and then his master again. But the man was paying him no more mind.

"Sit, dear," Jane said, placing a bagel and a glass of juice in front of the cushioned chair, "and eat your breakfast before it gets cold."

Daniel obeyed, feeling a little . . . he didn't even know what. He was sitting in *Carl fucking Whitman's* kitchen, eating gluten-free bagels on a cushioned chair at the same table as his master while wearing the first piece of clothing he'd ever actually owned.

When he tossed a longing glance at the *Washington Post*, still folded on the table, his master pushed it over to him without taking his eyes off the sports pages. "You don't ever have to ask," the master said. "Just put it back when you're done."

"Thank you, Master." The words were rote, but colored with stark surprise. On the news floor, he could take whatever reading material he wanted, but that was different. That was a *job*. This was . . . well, he supposed this was a job too. He just hadn't figured out his duties yet.

Daniel was halfway through A-4 when his master turned to him, nose wrinkled, and said, "You need a shower."

He folded the paper carefully, put it back exactly where he'd found it, and said, "Yes, Master." He almost added, *I'd like that very much*, but what did anyone care what he did or didn't like?

The master's eyebrows climbed a little. "Now?" he said, and Daniel realized his master's words had been the order, not just a statement preceding it.

"Sorry, Master. Of course." He stood up from the table and headed toward the slave bathroom, but his master stopped him with a hand around his wrist. He was thoroughly inured to being touched by others, and rarely gently, but something about this touch, this simple, almost hesitant touch, tripped his fight-or-flight instincts hard.

He did neither, of course. Didn't even have time to examine his response before the master said, "Use the guest shower. Three people sharing one bathroom is a bit much, don't you think?"

. . . No? Forty guys to a floor in NewWorld's West Side dorm, with one midsized bathroom—five sinks, five toilets, five shower heads—between them. They'd always made do just fine. But Carl obviously didn't want to hear that, and anyway it wasn't like he wasn't grateful for the gesture, so he muttered another "Thank you, Master," and changed course for the marble bathroom down the hall.

Once inside, he stripped behind the privacy of a closed door and stepped beneath the spray.

The soaps in this shower were expensive, boutique—the kind of thing you'd buy in a little shop in the East Village for twenty dollars a bar—and he wondered if his master had such fine tastes, or if this was Jane's hand he was seeing. He decided he didn't care as he turned into the three-headed spray and let it run down his face, his back, and the top of his head all at once, the heat melting the soreness from his muscles. He moaned and curled his toes into the heated tile.

"*Jesus,*" someone choked out.

Daniel whipped around to see his master standing naked just outside the stall glass, staring with his mouth open, his cock so hard it was bobbing against his belly.

Daniel stumbled back a step, bumping the wall, and swallowed hard. Closed his eyes and held his breath as the master slid the glass door open and stepped in next to him.

Only the thought of the strapping he'd so recently endured stopped him from bolting. He'd been through so many ugly things in his life, but this, this *thing* the master wanted from him, had easily been one of the most nightmarish, and it was so fucking *unfair* after all he'd done for NewWorld, all he'd given them, how well he'd served, and was it any fucking wonder he didn't believe in God anymore if *this* was his divine reward for—

A hand came to rest over his heart, and he startled so hard he hit the wall again, gasping his fear.

"Relax, Daniel. My God, you're like one of those shivery little wet dogs ridiculous women carry in their purses."

Daniel coughed out a frightened laugh—the image was remarkably astute. The master pulled his hand away, and Daniel sucked in a breath. A second later, the hand returned, complete with soaped-up loofah, and began to stroke across his chest.

"You keep up all this tension"—*stroke*—"you're gonna sprain something."

Yeah, maybe so. All those knotted muscles weren't doing his welted skin any favors, and God, he'd been so tired all the time lately. The loofah moved lower, brushed over both nipples. Daniel sucked in another shuddering breath and tried to make his fists unclench.

"Hey." *Stroke.* "*Hey.*"

The loofah left his skin, and two soapy fingers tilted his chin up toward his master's face. Daniel pried his eyes open and made himself look, shocked to see . . . *concern?* in those brown eyes.

"I'm not going to hurt you, you know."

The fingers disappeared, and Daniel dropped his chin again, suspecting that he and his master had two very different definitions of the word "hurt." He wanted to believe him, but he'd heard those words before, and they'd been a lie every time, even when the men speaking them had seemed kind. The loofah returned, low on his belly, and his eyes were drawn like magnets to his master's erection, much larger than Daniel's would be if his nuts weren't trying to crawl into his throat. All he could think of was why his master had bought him, what the man wanted so badly—or wanted to *hide* so badly—that he'd been willing to drop *millions* for it, and how long it would be before he lost his patience and simply took what he'd paid for.

The loofah brushed over Daniel's genitals, no faster or slower than it had over his torso, pushing no harder or softer. It was almost . . . clinical, Daniel thought, clenching his jaw but spreading his legs obediently when his master's hand nudged the inside of his thigh. The man squatted in front of him, his rock-hard cock bumping against Daniel's tense calf, his hands and eyes intent on the leg he was washing.

Then his master started on the other leg, leaning in close to reach across Daniel, that hard cock no longer just brushing but actually pressing against Daniel's calf. The master moaned at the same time Daniel did, but Daniel bit it back lest his master mistake the sound for desire. Of course, the master might not care one way or the other. He had no reason to.

No reason at all.

The master stood and said, "Turn around," his voice low and rough and as thick as the cock straining between his legs.

Daniel swallowed hard, breathed even harder. If he hyperventilated, maybe he'd pass out and . . .

No. No such luck. His body turned of its own accord, so accustomed to obeying orders that it didn't even check with his brain before moving. He braced his palms against the back wall of the stall, squeezed his eyes shut. He would *not* allow himself to beg, would *not* ask his master to stop, no matter how awful it was. He wasn't a child anymore, but there was still no way that giant cock could possibly fit where his master planned to put it. At least not without the agony he remembered, the blood, the tears, the way he couldn't sit or walk right or bear to use the toilet for days after. The way he could still *smell* them on him long after it was done, after he'd washed and washed again, the way he could feel their weight, scratchy hair and hot damp skin, pressing him down in his dreams. Would he be able to hold himself still through it now, or would the master, like those men from his past, have to pin him in place, shout at him, hit him until he stopped struggling?

His master stepped close, so near that Daniel felt the heat of him, even through the steam. Then a hand fell on his shoulder, and a soft, "Shhh," tickled his ear. Daniel wanted to believe the sound was meant to comfort, but maybe, like his first mistress, like the men she'd given him to, the master just didn't want to hear his fear.

Or worse, maybe he *did* want to hear it, and he was simply trying to unnerve Daniel.

The loofah made a single stroke down Daniel's bruised left shoulder, painful but bearable, and a trail of soap bubbles tickled down his back. Another stroke, toward the middle, then over the welts and cuts on his right shoulder. He hissed, muscles jumping and fingers flexing against the tile, and the loofah instantly withdrew. His master's bare hands took its place, soap-slicked and so, so gentle, working carefully around the worst and brushing feather touches over the rest.

It should've eased Daniel's mind, that careful touch. He knew it should've—a sadist wouldn't be so careful, would he? And yet still he trembled against the wall as those enormous hands trailed down his battered back, to his equally battered waist and hips. Daniel let his head drop between his arms, panted hard through clenched teeth. Maybe he even believed his master didn't mean to hurt him, but it hurt anyway, and it wasn't the road to Heaven that was paved with good intentions.

The next touch was the loofah again, which was better than the master's hands, but not by much. It stroked down to his ass—and Jesus, how long did it take to wash someone? How much longer would his master make him stand here, trembling beneath those hands, before the man took what he'd come for? For a moment, he wondered if the suspense wasn't worse than the actual deed would be—he knew some men *enjoyed* penetration, though he couldn't fathom how—but then his master's cock bumped his hip, and it felt like a steel fucking rod. Unbending, unyielding, cruel.

The master stepped away and adjusted the spray until the water washed the soap from Daniel's back. Every second that passed without skin against his skin, with hot water streaming in its place, Daniel unclenched a little more, but it was all undone a moment later when a large hand cupped his elbow and turned him around.

"You know," his master began, and from his blown pupils, flushed lips, and raging hard-on, Daniel was certain he was about to be scolded, berated, ordered to his knees. *You be a good little cunt now or I'll beat you senseless, you hear?* "Not to belabor the point, Daniel, but you really do need to calm down." And then he left, calling, "Stay in there as long as you like," as he toweled off and closed the door behind him.

Daniel stared at the suddenly empty bathroom, muscles locked and frozen, hot water streaming into his open mouth.

CHAPTER NINE

Daniel hid in the shower for a long time. There was no clock in there (there was, however, an in-shower radio, tuned to NPR when Daniel flipped it on), but it must have been half an hour, he figured, before the water went suddenly cold. He lunged for the tap with a curse and a flare of panic—he hadn't meant to lose so much time, hadn't meant to use all the hot water. What if the master wanted some?

His fingers had pruned. He dried off with a Turkish cotton towel four times the size of the ones in the dorms. His red toothbrush and a shaving kit were sitting on the sink, tagged with a little yellow sticky note that said simply, *Daniel*. The clothes waiting for him on the vanity also looked new—distressed jeans and a gently fitted black button-down shirt, navy watch-plaid boxers and a pair of socks. He wondered who had snuck in here to drop these things off, but what the hell, it felt like the whole damn world had seen him naked this week already. That he hadn't noticed someone come in was perhaps of slightly larger concern, but he couldn't quite bring himself to worry. He was tired and stressed and in pain, that was all.

He groomed and dressed slowly, half of him content to hide in here all day, the other half just *waiting* for the master to storm in, strike him, scold him for loafing. The shaving cream smelled fantastic. The clothes were soft and loose enough to be almost comfortable against his healing skin.

Finally, he ran out of excuses to stay inside his little marble cocoon. He wished he could find a reason to go to work today; he didn't know what having a heart attack felt like, but the morning had barely passed and already his throat felt tight and his chest hurt. How would he make it through a whole damn weekend of this?

One foot in front of the other, Daniel. You've lived through worse.

With a fortifying sigh, Daniel headed toward the living room. He found the master there, lounging on the couch, watching football on a huge TV. But the master didn't acknowledge or direct him. Not knowing what else to do, he stood off to one side, against the wall where he could watch the game (not that he had any idea what was happening), and where his master, if he so chose, could watch him.

The master finally turned his head, gave Daniel a slow, appreciative once-over, and went back to the game. Eight minutes into the first quarter. He'd probably be watching for a while.

At the two-minute warning, Jane and Dave came out of the slave suite, hand in hand. Dave said, "Back at three, Master."

The master waved them off with barely a glance. Was this a regular Saturday routine, then? Daniel ached to go with them, somewhere, anywhere that wasn't *here*. But they were gone before he could even think about working up the courage to so much as toss them a longing look, so he rocked back on his heels and resigned himself to an afternoon of sports.

How boring. *Epically* boring. He'd never been much good at doing nothing—not a lot of practice, after all. He stuffed his hands in his pockets, pulled them out to cross his arms, put them in his pockets again. Started writing questions in his head for the interview on Wednesday with that Tea Party asshat, who somehow simultaneously thought that slaves (rather than, say, automation) were to blame for the erosion of the blue-collar and unskilled job market but were also soulless godforsaken creatures who could only earn redemption through total dedication and lifelong service to society. On TV, another sack, still no score. God, didn't anything ever *happen* in this game? He was tired of standing, wanted some Tylenol. He shifted his weight from foot to foot.

"For God's sake, would you *sit*?"

The words cracked like a leather strap, and Daniel startled hard, apology spilling from his lips before the offense had even registered in his brain.

But his master didn't look particularly angry. Irritated, yes, but not angry. "You're not a dog, you know," the master added, sliding from irritated to . . . bemused? "I won't shoo you off the furniture. But

God help me, I may swat you on the nose with a rolled-up paper if you fidget even one more time."

Daniel believed him.

The couches formed an L around the coffee table, and he approached the unoccupied leg, sat stiffly on the edge of the middle cushion. The master followed him with his eyes, frowning slightly. Had he wanted Daniel to sit next to him? For a moment, the master looked like he might say something, but he only sighed and turned back to the game.

The new issue of the *Economist* lay on the coffee table. Did the master's never-have-to-ask rule apply to that as well, or only to the newspaper? It seemed absurd that the intention would be so narrow, so he reached for the magazine. Except . . . His hand froze, hovering over the coffee table. If the master had meant that he could read whatever he wanted, wouldn't he have said so? What if he was possessive about certain things? A producer had punished him just last month for borrowing hers without asking. He drew his hand back.

Really though, he was probably being ridiculous. His master seemed reasonable, maybe even kind. He wasn't some jerk with a chip on her shoulder and a shock prod she used behind Maxwell's back. Plus, the master had no reason to be jealous of Daniel—his ratings were three times higher, and he spent his broadcasts rubbing shoulders with A-list movie stars and influential politicians, not the unknown academics and policy wonks who made up Daniel's guest roster. Besides, the master clearly wasn't using the magazine right now. No harm done if he read it carefully. He leaned forward, reached for it again—

Unless, of course, his master saw fit to correct him for taking what wasn't his.

"God!" Another whip-crack exclamation from his master—the Lord's name in vain again, no less—and another hard startle from Daniel. "What did I say about the fidgeting?"

The master rocketed up from the couch, snatched the *Economist*, and rolled it into a tight tube. In two short, angry steps, he was in front of Daniel, magazine hand drawn back to his ear. Daniel squeezed his eyes closed and hunched his shoulders, waiting for the blows. At least they shouldn't hurt too much.

Or at all, apparently. Daniel popped his eyes open, surprised, when the magazine plopped into his lap. His master looked oddly apologetic.

"Hey," the master said, touching fingertips to Daniel's cheek and tilting his head up. "I told you, you don't have to ask, remember? I meant it. Books, papers, the TV, the bathroom, the kitchen, whatever; you live here now too. The only things off-limits are my laptop and the last slice of pie, okay?"

Daniel nodded, a hesitant smile creeping up his lips to match his master's own. That was more than okay, that was . . . "Thank you, Master, I— That's—" Despite his better judgment, he was starting to rewrite his initial impressions of his master. No way some sick fuck could be this nice, over and over and over again—and Daniel was pretty sure that was a truth and not just something he wanted to believe. "I mean, that's very kind of you. Thank you."

"Yeah, well, don't go saying that too loud," the master groused, grabbing his laptop off the coffee table and settling back on the couch. "You'll ruin my reputation."

The football game moved into the fourth quarter. Jane had returned about an hour ago with two canvas shopping bags and no partner ("The foreman called Dave in to work," she'd said to the master's raised eyebrow). She was puttering around in the kitchen now, baking something that made Daniel's mouth water.

Daniel was perhaps halfway through the *Economist*, starting to get restless with so much sitting around. His feet were jiggling. His ass was still sore, and he shifted his weight for perhaps the tenth time in as many minutes.

"So what do you think of that Bishops guy?"

The master was looking at him expectantly, as if he thought Daniel should be able to read his mind. Daniel put down the magazine and asked, "Master?"

"You know," the master said, eyes traveling between his computer screen and Daniel, one hand on his keyboard and the other twirling short, impatient circles in the air. "The British barrister campaigning to legalize manumission. That guy."

Daniel's eyes narrowed—was this . . . some kind of trap? Who the hell discussed slavery with slaves? "Nathaniel Bishops, you mean?"

The master turned to smile at Daniel. "Yes." He held the smile, as if waiting for a reply, so Daniel offered a tentative, "I think it's more likely to succeed in the UK than the US?" and the master went back to his laptop. He typed furiously for a few moments, then stopped and looked at Daniel again.

"Why?"

"Because the UK's core moral and scientific basis for slavery is a deeply embedded class system which, on very rare occasion, allows for upward mobility. Manumission in limited numbers wouldn't harm their economy or their social strata."

"And the US?" The master regarded him with open curiosity. "Ours isn't the same?"

Of course it wasn't, and surely the master knew that. There was no such history of classism here, only powerful religious roots, racist assumptions, and—for those whose faith in God didn't suffice— faith in science and the as-yet-unfound "slave gene" that gave people like him dampened affect, among a host of other behavioral and emotional issues. He opened his mouth to say so before Tim's words about confidential information popped into his head. *There's always a potential for corporate espionage. You have an obligation to protect the intellectual property of this company."* The master was obviously working on a story about this, so . . .

"I, I'm sorry, Master, but I can't— I mean, my handler says I'm not allowed to talk to you about anything that might . . . well, anything that might help you compete with them."

The master's eyebrows slowly knitted, and his hands tightened on his laptop casing. When he spoke, it was with audibly forced calm. "I know the rules of the lease I signed, Daniel. It's not like I'm going to torture you for company secrets. I just thought it might be interesting to talk politics with someone who understands both the policy *and* the reality of slavery. It's a rare opportunity, is all."

Daniel pinched his lips together and turned his eyes to his lap. That same anger he'd felt in his office yesterday surged back, and for a moment, he actually *hated* NewWorld—both for subjecting him to something so patently unfair, *and* for ever having made him a "rare opportunity" in the first place. Ignorance and bliss and all that . . . "I know, Master, and I really would love to, but they wo—"

"Fine." Though spoken softly, tightly, that single word reverberated like the harshest shout. "I get it. God knows what I'm paying for then, but fine. It's fine. Why don't you . . .?" The master tossed his hands up, clearly exasperated. Though he was a patient man on *Whitman Live*, he was also a passionate and occasionally vociferous one, not afraid to call a spade a spade or a lie a lie; Daniel was surprised the man had kept his anger reined in for as long as he had, or really that he'd bothered to at all. "I dunno. Do some"—more angry hand waving—"push-ups or something. You look like the kind of guy who'd enjoy that. Whatever, just . . . *stop fidgeting.*"

Eyeing the master warily, Daniel slid off the couch and to the floor beside the coffee table. Plenty of people watched him in the gym, sometimes quite openly, so it came as no surprise that his master might take pleasure from that too. He did one push-up, then another, grunting at the pain rippling through his right shoulder blade. But it was better than the alternative, and if the master's demeanor was any indication—Daniel could practically *smell* his irritation—the alternative was just one more slipup away.

He heard a loud sigh in the middle of the fourth push-up. "I didn't mean *right here*," the master said.

Daniel scrambled to his feet and sat back down. "I'm sorry, Master, I thought—"

"Doesn't that hurt with your back all bruised like that?"

Daniel blushed, realized he was tapping his fingers, and forced his hands to his sides. Answering a direct question wouldn't be seen as complaining, would it? Of course, even if it were, not answering would be worse. "Yes, Master."

Another loud sigh from his master. Daniel chanced a sideways look at the man and saw his head tilted back, a grimace on his broad face. "Jesus."

Daniel wondered if the master talked like that in public, how he'd ever climbed to the top of the career ladder while showing such little respect for God. Wondered why he felt so comfortable doing it in front of Daniel. Did he *know* somehow that Daniel didn't believe? Or did he just not care what he said in front of a slave, because who would believe one anyway?

The Master shoved his computer off his lap and dropped his head into his hands. "I need a neck rub," he grumbled. He leaned back on the couch, put his feet up on the coffee table. Glared at the football game, which had gone into overtime, and then at Daniel, who was able to pinpoint the exact moment when his master realized he had someone he could order to do that now. He sat up a little straighter and said, "Daniel, get over here."

Daniel bit back the sigh that so very much wanted to escape, replaced it with a neutral expression, and walked around the couch behind his master. He laid tentative hands on the man's broad shoulders—almost as tight as his own felt, he noted with surprise— and the master leaned back into the touch.

Daniel began to knead, reflecting bitterly that there was nobody now who would do this for him, that the few men who might have were relaxing in the InfoGlobe dorm half a city away, possibly never to be seen agai—

"Ow, not so hard!" The master jerked away, then leaned back into Daniel's hands again. Daniel realized he'd been squeezing. Furious. Trying to hurt.

"I'm sorry, Master." He really was sincere, if not for the right reason; he simply didn't want to be hurt back.

The master reached up to lay his own hand atop Daniel's. "That's okay." His fingers felt along Daniel's, tracing like a blind man's. "God, your hands are huge for a little guy."

The master's hand fell back to his lap, and Daniel began to knead again, paying more care. He hit a particularly tight knot, and the master moaned, let his head loll against Daniel's forearm. "Strong, too," the master breathed out. "Mmm, oh yeah, right there, Daniel, right—Yeah . . ."

Daniel grimaced, but did as he was told. A quick look over the master's shoulder revealed just how much the man was enjoying this massage. Not good, not good . . . How long would the master stay satisfied with Daniel's hands where they were? Especially since

Daniel's fingers were starting to cramp. He wouldn't be able to keep this up for much longer, and then the master would—

The master turned his head and pressed a lingering, closed-mouthed kiss to Daniel's right index finger.

Daniel froze, afraid to as much as twitch lest he accidentally encourage the master. He might well take what he wanted anyway, but Daniel wasn't about to encourage him.

The master's lips lifted a fraction, pressed down again. A low moan vibrated up from his throat and straight through to Daniel's finger. Daniel felt his chest seize, fought to force air into his frozen lungs.

The master's mouth opened, lips parting to suck in the tip of Daniel's finger, tongue brushing over the nail, the skin, teeth nibbling gently. For one horrible moment, Daniel was certain he'd cave in to the urge to pull his hand away—or worse, cave in to the signals his hand was trying so hard to send to the rest of him—but as if sensing this, the master's fingers curled around his wrist and held him in place. The grip was almost painfully gentle; Daniel thought he would have preferred a roughness, a forcing, over this imploring touch that asked-demanded he stay of his own accord. *Give* this of his own accord.

"Don't stop," the master moaned between wet little kisses, curling his fingers more possessively around Daniel's right wrist and tasting all the fingers he could reach.

Daniel swallowed hard and started to knead the master's shoulder again with his left hand, digging in to stop it from shaking. The master moaned, louder this time, and sucked Daniel's right index finger down to the first knuckle, in and out and in and out with shuddering, deliberate slowness. The fingers resting on Daniel's wrist began to stroke, and the master's left hand crept toward his lap.

Daniel panted, teeth clenched, willing his hands and feet to stay rooted with every ounce of stubborn strength he'd ever been accused of possessing, willing the rest of his body to ignore what was happening to his finger. Even if his master didn't want . . . Even if Daniel weren't so afraid of that, he couldn't—*wouldn't*—just smile and pretend he was happy. Not about this.

Fucking stupid, Daniel. Dangerous. You know that.

Sure. But knowing didn't change a thing.

The master released Daniel's finger, but only to lick a long stripe up the side of his hand.

Their eyes met. Both men froze. Though Daniel had thrown up his mask of indifference quickly—the best he could manage; eagerness was impossible—it hadn't been nearly quick enough.

Daniel dropped his gaze with an apologetic grimace, and the master slowly, slowly uncurled his fingers from Daniel's wrist and pulled away. He was still staring at Daniel—Daniel could feel it, though he could no longer see it, eyes fixed to the floor as they were. After several long, empty moments, the master announced to no one in particular, "I'll be in my room."

Daniel wiped his right hand on his pants after the master left, then gripped the couch tightly with shaking fingers, and wondered how five little words could taste so strongly of venom and sadness all at the same time.

CHAPTER TEN

Daniel had no idea how long he stood there, clutching at the back of the couch, trying to catch his breath as two talking heads discussed postgame on TV. He was pretty sure what the master had gone off to do. The big question, though, was what he'd do *afterward*, and how badly it would hurt.

A hand brushed his arm, and he jerked, stumbling back a step before forcing himself still; if the master meant to punish him, he'd be a fool not to face it.

"Easy, darling."

Just Jane. Daniel blew out the breath he'd sucked in and gave himself a little shake. The master was right—he was wound *way* too tight.

"Don't you worry none; he's just blowing off a little steam."

Jane's fingers slipped around his, peeling them gently from the couch cushion and holding his hand. It was . . . nice.

"I hurt his feelings." Or maybe his ego, but best not to say that out loud.

Jane pursed her lips, nodded slightly. Her face was serious, a little stern, but Daniel couldn't read it—was she upset with him? Upset with the situation? Merely concerned?

"Will he . . . ?" Daniel swallowed hard, and Jane's fingers tightened around his.

"Hurt you back?"

He nodded; Jane sighed.

"Come on, darling. Come make yourself useful." She tugged him into the kitchen, and even though she hadn't answered him, he went without resistance—with relief, even, eager for a distraction. When she sat him at the kitchen table and handed him a bag of apples and a peeler, his hands set to the monotonous work. He fought to untether his mind so that it might follow.

He was only halfway through the first apple when Jane, measuring and stirring at the counter behind him, asked, "You ever been in love, Daniel?"

"Yeah," Daniel answered, voice carefully flat lest he unleash something he couldn't contain. His hands finished with the first apple, picked up the next one. "Once."

Jane handed him a paring knife and a plate and said, "Core them. What happened?"

Daniel shrugged. "We got caught." He finished peeling the second apple, picked up the knife, and cored and sliced it in silence. But he could feel Jane's eyes boring into the back of his head, seeking more, and couldn't bring himself to ignore her. "NewWorld Media has a pretty strict policy about sexual relations. You can be ordered to breed, or apply for permission to breed, and if both parties are healthy, they'll probably say yes. But anything else? Forget it." He almost sliced open the tip of his finger, put down the knife, went back to peeling instead. "Spreads the *four Ds*, they say: distraction, dissension, disappointment, and disease."

Behind him, Jane snorted.

"His name was Victor. We lived together in the dorm on the West Side, same bunkroom. It was seven years back; I was still a field reporter. He was a sound tech. We used to sneak off into the bathroom, fool around. You only get three, maybe four minutes before the supervisors start getting suspicious, and even if you're quick, you've got to be careful; there are always people who will rat you out to get ahead, you know?"

Daniel paused, and Jane hummed an affirmation into the silence. There was something distant about the sound, something personal, and he felt certain that if he turned around and looked, he'd see bitterness, maybe even pain on her face. Instead he plucked another apple from the pile.

"We'd been going maybe eight, ten months, frantic handjobs in a toilet stall, that sort of thing. We knew some people were jealous of me. I don't know if someone reported us or if we just got careless, but it's not as if that mattered in the end."

Beside him, the pile of peeled apples had grown. His fingers were still working, working of their own accord. Jane's hand came to rest on his shoulder, squeezing gently. "What happened?"

Daniel grabbed another apple. He couldn't believe he was telling her this, hadn't told anyone but his mother. It wasn't safe to talk about it at InfoGlobe, and it hurt just to think about, even still. Maybe it really was true that slaves didn't feel like freemen did, but from where Daniel was sitting, that hardly seemed to matter now.

"Public beating. Whole dorm was there. Fifty strikes apiece, side by side. Next day they sent me off to cover some shit story, couple of hikers lost up in the Rockies. Twelve hours a day doing stand-ups in the snow, pretending like I wasn't in too much pain to think straight. They found the bodies on day three. I flew home so cold I was still shaking when the plane landed. Victor was gone. Never saw him again." He picked up the knife in a white-knuckled grip and mutilated the apple he'd just peeled. "Last memory I have of him is him screaming his throat raw as they beat him, begging them to stop hurting me. *Me.*"

Another mutilated apple. Jane stilled his wrist with one hand, divested him of the knife with the other. Her eyes were soft, damp with understanding. He didn't have the stomach for her compassion, not with this, so he dropped his gaze back to his sticky hands. "Anyway, I heard a couple years back that he's been working in the LA office for a while now."

Jane squeezed his wrist again, and he could see in her face that none of this was surprising or new to her. He wondered who she'd left behind, if she had children, if she knew her parents.

"I'm sorry," she said, and for a moment it looked as if she'd offer something more—some kindness or sympathy—so it came as a surprise when she said instead, "But at least you *enjoy* bedding men. Imagine how much harder this would be if you didn't."

Daniel blinked at her, realized his mouth was open and closed it. Opened it again when he couldn't hold back the clarification: "But I don't. Not like . . . What the master wants?" He shook his head, closed his eyes against sense memory over two decades old. "It's terrible. Bled me worse than a strapping."

Jane scowled—some strange mix of sympathy and reprobation. "Do you *know* what the master wants? Did you ask? Did he tell you? Maybe he'll want something you like."

Huh. Yeah, maybe. He doubted it, though, considering how much money had changed hands for him. Not to mention that being attracted to men was not at all the same thing as being attracted to one specific man. Still, cold comfort, he supposed, was better than no comfort at all. Besides, this couldn't be easy for Jane *or* Dave; when the master was unhappy, so was everybody else, and that was nobody's fault but his.

"Look, darling," Jane said, her expression softening but still nowhere near soft. "The master may not be pushing you now, but if you keep giving him the cold shoulder, he's gonna up and bust one day. And that man has a temper; you *don't* want to see it pointed at you."

And just what, exactly, did that mean? "But I thought . . . I mean, has he—?"

"No, course not. Master's never laid a hand on either of us the whole five years we've been here. But then"—she gave Daniel another hard, appraising look—"he didn't buy *us* for laying on hands, now did he."

Daniel winced. He'd taken Jane for softer, not capable of such brutal honesty, yet she'd ambushed him twice in as many minutes. She was trying to help, he knew, but it didn't make him feel any better. Nor did it solve his problem. He still couldn't bring himself to offer up freely what the master wanted, and apparently the master couldn't bring himself to take it. Or maybe he didn't *want* to take it; maybe he wanted to be wanted in return. But that was never going to happen. Where, then, did that leave them?

"Anyway," she said, full once again of the sunny cheer with which Daniel had come to associate her, "that's just my advice. You can take it or leave it, of course." She turned back to the counter, and silverware clinked against a plate. "You should, however, take this."

Before he could ask what "this" was, she'd traded a fresh-baked brownie for his half-sliced apples, ruffled his hair, and began to core the apples herself.

They sat in silent companionship for some time, Jane cooking a variety of the master's favorite foods for dinner ("He's an easy one to placate; you just gotta know which buttons to push"), Daniel reading the paper and helping her when she asked.

Dave came home around 5:30, too sweaty and grimy for the hug he wanted. Jane sent him straight to the shower and, with a put-out sigh, cleaned up the muddy trail he'd left behind.

The master joined them at six, just as Jane was putting plates to the table. He smiled at everyone, said, "Smells great!" and waved Daniel to the chair beside him.

Daniel sat warily, studying the master for clues: He was smiling on the outside, but it looked like it hurt him a little. His body was loose, but his eyes were tense. Putting on a friendly face, Daniel thought, to cover his frustration. Trying to pretend the last few days hadn't happened. Trying to start again.

Well, Daniel could certainly play that game. If the master was willing to grant him such a kindness, he'd be a fool not to take it.

Jane served them, and the master attacked his steak, grunting in approval. Daniel, however, found himself without an appetite, despite the richness of the food. He made a volcano of his mashed potatoes, filled it with gravy, carved runnels into its side with his fork. Cut the heads off his asparagus and arranged them into a neat rows by size.

"Don't you like it?" the master asked.

Daniel looked up, startled. Somehow, he'd half forgotten he wasn't alone with his food.

"I spoiled his appetite with brownies," Jane said from where she'd been hovering by the counter, waiting to see if the master needed anything. Daniel wondered when she got to eat, where Dave was, if they would have the privilege of enjoying the food he was taking so entirely for granted.

The master's ears perked, and he smiled. "You made brownies?"

Safely out of the master's eye, Daniel picked up his knife and cut a bite of steak. It was easier to eat than to come up with words that wouldn't upset the man. Plus, he had to admit the food was damn good—he hadn't had steak since that lunch interview at Michael's with the writer from *GQ*. And that whole meal had been seasoned with contempt, with hard stares from patrons and slights and sneers from the waiters—both free and not free—at the presence of a slave in such a fine establishment.

There was no contempt now, but tension, expectation, and disappointment tasted just as bitter. The master was not good at hiding his feelings or starting over. In fact, as he turned his attention back to Daniel and his brownie-induced smile faded to a scowl, it seemed as if he'd even forgotten his intention to try. Daniel took another bite of steak and tried to look as grateful as he knew he should be.

"So," the master began again, "you can't talk politics, you can't talk news. What *can* you talk about?"

Daniel knocked in the rim of his volcano with his fork, and streams of lava-gravy overtook all his little asparagus people. He speared one and ate it, shrugging so cautiously it felt like a cringe. Admittedly, it might have been. He knew the master would not be pleased with his silence, but he could think of nothing better.

The master dropped his fork to his plate with a clatter. "You *can* talk?"

"Of course, Master." Daniel carved new lines into his mashed potatoes, scooping up some to eat when the master glared at him.

"No, that wasn't—" The master's voice rose in clear frustration, maybe even anger. "I mean, you can *talk*. Anytime you want. About anything. God knows you don't seem to be good for much else."

Daniel froze with his fork halfway to his mouth. So much for starting fresh.

"And while we're clearing things up," the master added, words a low rumble, "your place, at night, is in my bed."

Daniel barely managed to contain his grimace at the master's bluntness. He didn't like to think of himself as a companion, but there it was, laid out as naked as he'd surely be in a few hours.

"I don't care what time you get home, I don't care if I'm already asleep; if I *ever* wake up and find you on the floor again—"

Daniel dared a glance at the master. Beneath all the bluster, he thought he saw hurt, and confusion, and maybe even an apology, but of course such things could never be voiced. Daniel couldn't imagine what the master would have to be sorry for, anyway; he was being much more patient than Daniel had any right to expect.

"I understand, Master."

The master nodded, but kept his eyes fixed on Daniel's face. Waiting for him to say something, no doubt, to take advantage of his newly explained freedom.

But Daniel's mind was blank. For God's sake, he talked for a living—why couldn't he think of anything now?

"You know what?" the master said, voice as tight as his grip on his silverware. "Just—eat your food."

Having given up on Daniel, the master turned to Jane and conversed with her instead. Their discussion was perfectly cordial, but the tension around the master's eyes had seeped into the rest of his large frame, and despite what Jane had said earlier, Daniel couldn't help but wonder if things might go very, very south once the master got him alone tonight.

The master perked up quite a bit when Jane broke out the brownies—*easy to placate, indeed,* Daniel thought with a fleeting smile. He had to admit they were pretty damn good; Daniel had a second one, and by the time the master had polished off his third, he was looking like he might be ready to try starting again, well, *again*.

"All right." The master stood up from the table and rubbed his belly, which was rounded just a little with middle age and triple-brownie desserts. He smiled at Daniel, a gesture so surprising that it startled Daniel into smiling back. The master walked past him, brushing his side on the way, and started rooting around in the cabinet beneath the television. "How about a little *Holy Grail*?"

According to the master's raised eyebrows, this was not a rhetorical question. Too bad Daniel had no idea what he was talking about. "A little what, Master?"

Those raised eyebrows knitted tight. "*Monty Python and the Holy Grail*?" Daniel shook his head, and the master's face knitted up even tighter. "Cult classic? Only the funniest spoof of all time?"

"I'm sorry, Master, I mostly only get to watch what's in the dorm library. They don't have that one."

"Well, Jesus," the master said mildly, popping in the DVD and plopping on the couch. "Get your skinny ass over here and enjoy the show."

The master held his arm out, and Daniel blanked his face before settling on the cushion next to him. This close, the man made Daniel feel tiny, fragile, even though he was no such thing. At least the master kept his arm to himself, laid across the back of the couch several inches from Daniel's shoulders.

When the master smiled at him and said, "Lean back, relax," Daniel was actually glad to have the beating as an excuse to *keep* that arm several inches away: "It hurts my back," he said, and the master seemed to accept that at face value.

The movie was . . . well, *stupid*, frankly, though the master seemed to find it sidesplittingly hilarious, and even Daniel was willing to admit that maybe he was just too tense for this level of silliness. Besides, the current running underneath it wasn't funny at all, and after that scene with the king and the "I didn't vote for you" peasants, it was no wonder to Daniel why he'd never been allowed to watch the movie before. The *real* wonder was why the master thought this appropriate viewing. Was he trying to tell Daniel something? Or was he actually as dense as he sometimes seemed?

Then the damn movie got even less funny when, some endless stretch later, the master dropped his arm onto Daniel's shoulders in the middle of a particularly loud guffaw and yanked him close.

"This just never. Gets. Old!" the master said between laughs, squeezing hard enough to make Daniel squeak and not stopping until they were practically snuggling, Daniel curled in toward the man, his head smushed against master's shoulder and his face nearly turned into the master's neck. Then the vise let up and his master's arm curled gently around his head, petting his hair and tracing his earlobe with a finger. "Having a good time, Daniel?" he asked, nuzzling his nose against Daniel's scalp.

"Yeah," Daniel lied, the sound muffled by the master's shirt. He felt a little shiver run through the master when his breath puffed against the man's neck, and then the master's other hand crept onto his thigh, began to stroke back and forth, coming a little closer to his groin on each pass. Daniel didn't dare pull away, but nor did he open up to him.

"I thought you'd appreciate the bit about the coconuts," the master said, his voice dropping in a way that might have been coldly dangerous or hotly sensual. Daniel thought it was the second, but he knew how easily it might become the first, especially since he had no idea what the master was talking about.

"Uh, yeah," he said again, hoping it would be enough.

The master's hands stilled on his body, the one around his head fisting in his hair and tugging until Daniel looked him in the eye. He wasn't smiling anymore. Not even close. But it wasn't anger Daniel saw in its place—no, it was that same strange mixture of bluster, hurt, and confusion he'd seen at dinner, that he was so ill equipped to deal with in any way.

"You have no idea what I'm talking about, do you." The words were flat and accusatory and even, Daniel thought, wounded. Daniel tried to drop his gaze, but the master's fist tightened in his hair until he winced (and then loosened, he noticed, immediately), holding him still.

"No, Master," he sighed. "I'm sorry; I didn't mean to lie. I'll just . . ." He slid out from under the master's arm, off the couch and to his knees, and started to unbutton his shirt. Lying was never less than five with the strap at NewWorld, sometimes as many as twenty if the lie was particularly egregious. Given the shape he was currently in, even one would set him screaming, but he deserved this. Deserved this and more, the way he'd been—

"What are you *doing*?"

Daniel's fingers stilled on a button. The rest of him froze, too; even his breath caught in his lungs.

"I lied, Master."

"Yes, and?"

"And . . ." God, he could barely bring himself to say it. If the master hadn't planned to beat him, he certainly didn't want to give him any ideas. But he was waiting, impatient for an answer, and Daniel would *not* lie a second time. "And I assumed you'd wish to punish me."

A loud sigh behind him, then a foot nudging his hip. "Get up. Turn around, look at me."

And there it was, that same expression all over again—except worse this time, with outrage and horror piled atop the rest.

"And for God's sake, button your damn shirt. I'm not— I don't—" The master pulled off his glasses, scrubbed his face with both hands, put them back on. Picked up the remote to stop the movie, then tossed it on the couch as if he were mad at *it* and not Daniel. "You know what?" He stood, clearly angry, and Daniel couldn't help it, he took a single step back. "I've seen this movie a thousand times. The end is stupid. I'm going to bed."

Daniel watched him leave, mouth open, the metallic taste of adrenaline strong on the back of his tongue. The master's bedroom door slammed so hard the clock fell off the wall. Daniel hung it up again with shaking fingers. It was only 8:15.

CHAPTER ELEVEN

For a while, Daniel was able to pretend all was well. He retrieved the remote from where the master had thrown it, flipped through the channels until he came across some terrible reality show about a deaf couple with three not-deaf kids who walked all over them like they were slaves instead of parents. The little brats didn't even know sign language. It wasn't long before the whole thing grew unbearable, and he shut it off, picked up the *Economist* instead, and started reading where he'd left off.

But his mind kept turning back to the master, to the closed door at the end of the hall. What would happen when he went through it tonight? Could he wait until the master was asleep and then tiptoe in? Would he get away that easily, or was the master a light sleeper? Or worse, was the master *waiting* for him? Should he just go, get it over with? When had Japan gotten a new prime minister? He really *hadn't* been paying attention this week, had he?

"You should go to him."

Daniel looked up, startled, to see Jane returning the DVD to its case and putting it back in the cabinet. How long had she been standing there?

"He can't possibly want me around," Daniel said into his magazine. "He thinks I hate him."

"Well, then." Jane stepped close and plucked the magazine from Daniel's unresisting fingers. "It's time to go disabuse him of that notion, don't you think?"

She was right. He knew she was. If the master meant to punish him, it would be foolish to try to delay it. And if the master meant to use him, making him wait would only lead to more anger, frustration, alienation, and hurt—which would make it so much worse for Daniel when it finally happened. He was exploiting the master's kindness, stretching the master's patience too thin. Rather than rejoicing in his master's clear desire to arouse and interest Daniel, he was taking advantage of it, being deliberately obtuse, closing his eyes and—like a child—thinking that would somehow make the world go away.

But that didn't work when I was eleven, and it sure as hell isn't going to work now.

When Jane pulled out a vacuum cleaner and started banging his feet with it, he took the hint and left for the master's bedroom.

Uneasy with barging in, he knocked first, only opening the door when the master shouted, "For God's sake, stop knocking and just get in here!"

Daniel's hands were shaking, so he stuffed them in his pockets, stood shuffling in the doorway, and peeked up at the master through lowered eyes.

The master was in pajamas that would have made Daniel laugh if he weren't so tense—green flannel covered in footballs, helmets, goalposts, and yard lines—sitting against the headboard and reading Nathaniel Bishops again. Or maybe still.

"Hey." The master's voice was light but strained, just as it had been at dinner. "So I leased this slave, guy named Daniel Halstrom? Brilliant, funny, sharp tongue, quick on his feet, puts everyone at ease in a heartbeat. You seen him? Maybe you could go get him for me; I think we'd get along great."

"I—" Daniel realized he had no idea how to finish that sentence and shut his mouth before he got himself into even more trouble. He took a hesitant step forward, closed the door behind him; if things got ugly, he didn't want Jane to have to hear it.

The master marked his place and put his book on the nightstand, never taking his eyes off Daniel. "You're not going to tell me that man's all an act, are you? Because I don't believe it, I can't believe that's all some . . . *front*. I mean look at me; I'm like that on TV too. Am I so different here?"

Daniel shook his head, worked up the courage to take a few more steps toward the bed. "No, Master." Except for the putting people at ease part. Daniel had quite possibly never been *less* at ease. But he couldn't say that, so instead he offered, "That's, that's me. I mean, when I'm—" *Relaxed. Unafraid. In my element.* But he couldn't say any of that either, of course, and didn't know what he could possibly say in its place.

"Right. Which is why I figured—" The master clamped his mouth shut, grimaced. He looked almost . . . disappointed? Had he thought they'd be . . . what? Equals, somehow? That they'd sit in bed together and commiserate about the joys and tribulations of being public personalities at the top of their related fields? That they'd laugh and share stories and become best friends? Could he possibly be that delusional? Or was he just that clueless?

"Come here." The master patted the bed. He looked more determined now than upset, and Daniel sat stiffly, dropping his eyes to his hands. He could feel the master's gaze on him—face, shoulder, hips, hair.

"You gonna sleep in your new clothes?"

"No, Master," Daniel said, understanding that it wasn't a question. He stood, stripped quickly before he lost his nerve, folded the clothes on a nearby chair, and slid back into bed. He mirrored the master, sitting up against the headboard, covers pulled up to his waist. He was grateful for the blanket, felt a little less exposed that way, but still sat as close to the edge as he could without falling off.

The master sighed, clearly aggrieved, then stood to strip himself. Daniel fixed his eyes on the blanket as the master pulled off his top.

"No," the master said. "Look at me."

Inside, Daniel hedged, but his head turned by itself. His eyes trailed up the master's broad chest, thick with hair just starting to gray, then down, following the master's hands as they pulled off pants and boxers in one motion to reveal that formidable erection. Formidable *everything*—nothing about the master was small or delicate or weak.

Though reluctant to admit it, even to himself, Daniel suspected he'd have found that attractive under different circumstances. That he *would've* liked the master, commiserated and laughed with him, if they'd both been slaves. But they weren't, were they.

He knew he should get up, touch the man, maybe drop to his knees and swallow him down. Maybe if he was good enough, he could get the master off before the man could even think about fucking him.

But what if he wasn't good enough? In fact, he almost certainly wouldn't be. He'd always viewed such pleasures as a gift, an act borne of—well, if not love, then at least deep affection. Could he perform without such feelings? If ordered, perhaps, but to *offer*? No. Besides, he had little experience and no formal training. The master would tire of his clumsiness, turn him over and . . .

And rip me open, and expect me to like it anyway.

The master left his clothes in a heap and climbed back into bed, pushing the covers away and leaving Daniel as exposed as he was. He lay back against two pillows, half-reclined, much closer to Daniel than he'd been before. His body angled toward Daniel ever so slightly, cock jutting toward Daniel's hip.

Daniel couldn't help but stare at it.

The master stared back.

"You seem a little slow," the master said at length, then went silent again.

Daniel didn't think that was some kind of hidden question, but it might have been a complaint, so he ventured, "I'm sorry, Master."

The master just snorted and wrapped one giant hand around his giant dick.

Daniel's eyes, wide and hot, raced back to his own lap.

"No," the master growled. "No, damn it, look at me!"

Daniel swallowed audibly, trying to force his heart back down his throat. The master was pumping himself: long, slow strokes with a tightly fisted hand. If he felt any pleasure, his face did not reflect it. He was glaring at Daniel, just as he had at dinner, as he had during the movie. But this time, overtop the anger, the frustration, the confusion, Daniel saw incredulity as well.

"I'm confused," the master said, his fist still moving over his cock. "Do you *want* me to hit you? Would that make you feel better?"

"N-no, Master, of course not!"

"Do you not understand anatomy, then?" The question was sharper, angrier than the one before it, and the master's hand sped up to match. Daniel winced; there was violence in that fist, straining to break free. Maybe it already had. "Do you get how this"—the master thrust his hips at Daniel, face bent into a grimace, wrist twisting hard over his cock—"works?"

"Y-yes," Daniel said, reaching out with one hand to do what the master so clearly wanted before the man beat him senseless. *It's just a handjob, Daniel, just a handjob; it doesn't have to mean something.*

The master smacked his fingers away with a growl and went back to jacking himself. The sound of fist against flesh grew louder, the smell of anger and arousal filling the room. Daniel knew that scent all too well.

"Because I *thought* you had a working one of your own," the master said, "and that maybe"—*jerk*—"just *maybe*"—*jerk*—"you'd be smart enough to figure it out!"

Daniel inched his hand ever so slightly back toward the master's lap, offering his service again. "I—"

"God!" the master shouted, his fist nearly a blur over his cock, his face twisted with bitterness, with empty, unsatisfying pleasure. "Stop talking! There's no staff here to write your witty repartee, and oh, my bad, I seem to have left my teleprompter in the other room! Lord knows you can't seem to string three words together without it— No, no! Look at me. *Look at me!*"

Daniel realized he'd pulled into a huddle, his face tucked into the cradle of his arms. He forced himself to unclench, to turn his eyes back to the master's cock, to the white-knuckled hand jerking short and furious near the head. Any second now, that hand would be turned on him, he was sure of it.

"Because apparently," the master snapped, picking up right where he'd left off, as if he weren't jacking himself so hard he'd probably leave bruises, as if his cock weren't connected to the rest of him in any way, "that mouth really *is* too pretty for intelligent discourse. No wonder I beat you so badly in the ratings every day; all you do is stutter! And Ben Cheng is too busy daydreaming about burying his cock up your ass—which, no doubt, you have magically somehow *never realized*—to figure out that there's obviously *nothing there* beneath that shiny blond head of yours! But *oh*, that doesn't matter, because all you have to do is *sit there* and everyone falls all over you! And *you*, all 'look at me in my custom-tailored suits that show off my perfect ass and bring out the blue in my oh-so-bright eyes,' hiding your bracelets in jackets worth more than most schmucks make in a month because they aren't *good* enough for you, they can look but never touch, oh no, because you're *above* us mere mortals, you're—"

The master's orgasm strangled his next words, turned them into a grunt that sounded almost painful. It seemed to catch him by surprise, and he looked pissed at it, pissed that even a fleeting moment's pleasure had dared to interrupt his tirade. It caught Daniel by surprise too—how could such a thing bloom from such roughness, such fury?—splattering the sheets and his shaking hip. And with both the master's hands free, would that roughness, that fury, be unleashed on him through something more bruising than words?

"Oh, look," the master drawled, no longer shouting but each word still dripping with venom. "Do you like my shot?" The master drew a finger through the line of cum on Daniel's hip, wiped it on Daniel's stomach. "What, no charming comments, Halstrom? No banal proclamations disguised as wit and wisdom?"

Daniel had no idea how to answer. He didn't really think the master wanted an answer anyway, which was good, because he was probably trembling too hard to speak, so far past frightened that he'd moved right on to numb. He dared a look at the master's face, and the master glared back, hard and steady.

Then all at once the man seemed to deflate, to unclench, to actually become *less* somehow.

"Well," the master said, all the anger leached out of his voice, leaving only weariness and perhaps a hint of . . . wry amusement? "How about a washcloth, at least?"

Daniel was out of bed so fast he thought he made a draft.

He took perhaps a little longer in the bathroom than he should have, washing the sweat from his face while he waited for the water to run hot. When he returned to the bedroom, the master—much to Daniel's relief—reached for the washcloth, leaving Daniel with no confusion about whether he should clean the man himself.

When the master was done, he tossed the washcloth on the floor without a second glance. Daniel remained standing by the side of the bed, hopped up on adrenaline that he ached to spend five or six miles jogging off, worried that the master would burn it off for him with a strap, or worse, those enormous fists.

The master settled back against his pillows, pulling up the covers and patting the empty spot beside him. "Well, come on," he said, reaching up to turn out the light, and though every last cell in Daniel's body screamed at him to run, to hide, to *get away*, he obediently climbed beneath the blankets. He did, however, curl up on his side away from the master, counting that as a win.

Until the master rolled over and spooned up next to him, pressing skin to skin from ankle to neck and wrapping a tight arm around his middle. Daniel yelped at first contact, but made no struggle.

"Oh, for fuck's sake." The master sighed into the back of Daniel's neck, pressing his lips there with what seemed like affection—and wasn't *that* just too weird for Daniel to even begin to get his head around. "I'm a forty-two-year-old man who just came in his own hand. I assure you your virtue is safe for the night. Now go to sleep."

Sleep. Yeah, right. The hand at his stomach slid up to the jointure of his shoulder and neck, kneaded with gentle force, then resettled against his belly. Soon after, he heard soft little almost-snores, and managed a first, hesitant attempt to unknot his body—so hard to do with the hot, heavy reminder pressed to his back, draped over his side, breathing softly against his neck. But sometime near dawn, he managed to convince himself that the danger—for that moment, at least—had finally passed, and he slipped into a fitful sleep.

Daniel woke perhaps an hour later, sweaty and sore, the master plastered to him like a sheet of hot, heavy cellophane. He stretched carefully, trying to ease his way out from under the arm and leg wrapped over him without waking the master, or at least to roll onto his back and kick the covers off, but it seemed the master was too light a sleeper.

"What'd I say about fidgeting," the master half grumbled, half slurred. His arm tightened around Daniel's middle.

Daniel tensed, ventured a careful, "Sorry, Master. I was hot."

The arm disappeared just long enough to flip back the bit of blanket covering Daniel, then returned. "*Now* can you hold still and let me sleep?"

"Yes, Master," he said, even as his legs shuffled beneath the master's much heavier one, cramped from the weight and too much time spent in the same position.

An angry sigh puffed across the back of his neck. "What, you gotta piss or something?"

The master sounded more fully awake now, and also quite irritated. The hostility made Daniel wonder if he hadn't simply imagined that brief moment of affection last night after . . . well, after whatever the hell exactly that was. Sarcastic tirade? Angry masturbation session? Either way, he counted himself lucky to have come out of it without any new bruises. Unless the ones to his ego counted; if the master really felt that way about him, why'd he bother to lease him?

The fingers resting on his stomach clenched, curling in with warning force. "You plan on answering me sometime before the end of the year?"

Shit. He'd forgotten the question. "I . . ." He hedged, thinking furiously back. What the hell was wrong with him? Sure it'd been a long night, a fucking *eternal* weekend, but that was no excuse for— Oh. Bathroom. Right. "Sorry, yes," he lied, seeking escape, however brief, from the clutches of the prickly man behind him.

The master let loose another sigh, and Daniel swore he could *hear* the accompanying eye roll. But the arm and leg atop him disappeared, and then a hand between his shoulder blades gave him a not-so-gentle nudge that reawoke the pain of fading bruises. "Hurry up. Goddamn six-million-dollar cuddle, I damn well plan to enjoy it."

It didn't seem to Daniel that the master was enjoying much of anything just now—in fact, a quick glimpse of the master's face in the early light revealed not just irritation but also, he thought, *disgust*. Obviously, the man was furious with him. The "six-million-dollar cuddle" had felt deliberately punitive, even a little cruel, as if the master knew it was the last thing Daniel wanted. It was equally possible, of course, that the master didn't give a damn what Daniel wanted and simply meant to take at least a little of what he'd paid so much for, angry or not.

Whatever the case, Daniel was glad to be away from it, even if only for a few moments. He didn't have to piss, but he forced himself anyway, just in case the master was listening, then washed his hands and face, shivering slightly as sweat dried on his skin in the cool air. He wanted to stretch, shower, go for a run, come back and sleep for twelve solid hours. But none of that was an option anymore, and the master was waiting none too patiently for Daniel's return. He didn't dare dawdle.

Daniel left the bathroom and climbed back into bed. Before he'd even had a chance to settle, the master tugged him into his arms, pressed his chest to Daniel's back and wove his legs between Daniel's own. Despite the man's earlier assertion that he was too old to come twice in one night, proof against it pressed hard along the crack of Daniel's ass. Not forcing, not even asking—but still very much *there*.

It reminded Daniel of those men who'd used him so carelessly at his old mistress's shop. Worse, it reminded Daniel of sneaking embraces with Victor in the bathrooms of the InfoGlobe dorm, of Victor sneaking up behind him and wrapping arms around his chest. Feeling Victor's lips at his nape, Victor's cock nudged up against him, begging for attention from his hands or mouth. And surely it was only those memories making his skin hum, bringing the blood to his cock as he lay in another man's arms.

Shame heated his cheeks anyway, and he cursed his errant body for pulling shit like that in such a dangerous situation.

"Better?" the master asked, but it sounded a lot more like a demand than a question. So even though Daniel was hot and uncomfortable again—in more ways than one—and the master's tight, skin-to-skin press was painful against healing welts, and *God*, he didn't even know where to begin with how freaked out he was with that erection trying to worm between his ass cheeks, he thought it prudent not to argue. "Yes, Master."

"Then for heaven's sake, stop squirming and go back to sleep. There's only one good reason for you to keep me up at night, and this sure as fuck ain't it."

Daniel took a breath to apologize again, but the master cut him off with a tight squeeze around his middle. "Just *be quiet*. Not another word. I'm sick of hearing you, and I'm sure as fuck not gonna fall for your little endearing-stutter routine anymore. So just . . . Sleep. Now. Before you really piss me off."

Daniel felt certain it was much too late for that, but nevertheless, he did as he was told.

CHAPTER TWELVE

When next Daniel awoke, he was blissfully alone. He didn't remember falling back to sleep, though obviously he had. He'd also somehow managed to sprawl across the entire bed. He peered at the clock and nearly panicked. *2:37 p.m.?* Jesus! He hadn't slept that late since . . . since . . . Well, the last time he had, he'd probably been too sick to remember it. And even though he knew he had no real place here, nothing to do, nobody who needed him, he still couldn't shake the feeling that he'd overslept, shirked some duty, and would be in trouble for it.

But nobody came in shouting or wielding shock prods. In fact, nothing happened at all. He heard no sounds from outside the closed door, and actually suspected he might be alone in the apartment. A strange thought, vaguely frightening, yet also quietly liberating; if ever he'd been alone—truly alone—even once in his lifetime, it predated his earliest memories.

He climbed out of bed in a strange slow motion, tiptoed to the door, and cracked it open, absurdly afraid that even the slightest noise might break the spell.

The hallway was empty. So were the guest bed and bath, and the living room, and the kitchen. The slave quarters were abandoned, too.

Back in the kitchen, he spun a slow circle and thought, *I can do anything.*

He entertained the idea of running away for about 0.6 seconds, but of course, the damn GPS chip buried behind his left collarbone would make that impossible. Not to mention that even just a ghost of the memory of what he'd endured the one and only time he'd tried, on a trip to Denmark a few months after they'd taken Victor away, left him nauseous and shaking. He'd make them kill him before he'd ever suffer through that again. Besides, where would he hide in the States, even if he could somehow ditch the chip? Everyone knew his face here.

Forcing such thoughts from his head, he grabbed a brownie, idly opening cabinets and drawers as he ate. Silverware. Cookware. Plates and glasses. Little kitchen hand tools he hadn't used since NewWorld bought him: corkscrew, can opener, measuring spoons, one of those plastic grippy things for opening stubborn lids. A drawer full of pens, paper, rubber bands, dozens of restaurant matchbooks . . . a Hot Wheels car? His first mistress's son had played with those, would sometimes make Daniel watch but never let him play too. This one was bright red, no longer than his thumb. He pulled it out and backed it up along the counter, released it, and watched it fly. Again, and again, until it rolled right off the counter and clacked to the floor.

Daniel retrieved the car with a startled curse, terrified for a moment that he'd broken it. But the toy looked just the same as before. He put it back where he'd found it, between the paper clip chain and the hot pink Koosh Ball.

Still hungry, he opened the fridge, reeling at the sheer magnitude of choices within. He realized maybe a minute later that he was just standing there staring with the door open, and also that he was cold—he hadn't bothered to put clothes on, though for once he had no reason to be self-conscious about that. He grabbed the milk. Took a shifty-eyed look around the apartment and, confirming it still empty, drank straight from the carton.

God, that felt *good*.

Thirst slaked, he found ice cream in the freezer, whipped cream in the fridge, sprinkles and fudge sauce in the pantry. He crumbled another brownie over all that and ate his sundae sprawled naked on the couch as he scrolled through the master's DVR.

He discovered about halfway through his sundae and an old episode of *The Simpsons* in which his master had guest-starred that his eyes were significantly bigger than his stomach, at least when it came to something as sweet and rich as brownie sundaes. He wasn't accustomed to having more food than he could finish, and so found himself with the curious dilemma of what to do with his leftovers. In the end, worry at being punished for wastefulness overshadowed worry at eating ice cream for breakfast (the master had, after all, said more than once that he could help himself to anything at any time), so he put his leftovers back in the freezer.

Sticky with dried sweat and chocolate sauce, he decided on a shower. The bathroom was more extravagant than he remembered it being, the water more relaxing. He sat on the heated marble bench inside the stall, three adjustable heads pounding him with water, and nearly let himself drift to sleep. What a difference it made to make the *choice* to shower, and to know the master wouldn't be barging in to join him.

He stayed in the stall a long time, careful only not to let the water run cold. His track pants and a T-shirt, socks and underwear sat clean and folded on the master's dresser. He put them on, then wandered back into the kitchen to finish his leftover sundae.

And that was how Jane and Dave found him ten minutes later, sitting at the kitchen table, reading the Sunday *Times* and licking melted ice cream off the side of his hand.

"Glad to see you're settling in," Jane said around a chuckle and an armful of groceries. "Though God knows how you keep that body eating so much junk."

Jane put her packages down on the counter, gestured Dave to do the same, and then shooed the man off to their bedroom with a silent glance and a peck on the cheek. Once he was gone, she turned her full attention back to Daniel, sitting down next to him and giving him a careful, serious once-over.

"What," he asked flatly, weirded out by how hard she was studying him and unfairly angry that she'd ended his time alone. But then it clicked: surely she'd heard all that shouting last night. "I'm fine," he said, scraping the last of his ice cream from the bowl. "He didn't hurt me, if that's what you're worried about."

"Good," she said, her bright smile returning. "Good."

He stood to rinse his bowl in the sink, but Jane snatched it from his fingers and did it for him. "Sit, darling."

He wanted to tell her she didn't have to wait on him, but surely she already knew that, and she might even find it insulting. Instead, he asked, "Where's the master?" not really sure he wanted to know.

Jane shrugged, washed his bowl, put it in the drain board, and wiped her hands on a dish towel. "He left before noon wearing a great big frown that screamed *don't talk to me.* I thought it best to listen. Maybe he went to the office. Maybe to a friend's. Wouldn't be surprised if he was out getting drunk; he don't do it often, but . . ."

But I pissed him off, and now he can't even stand to look at me.

"Anyway, I thought I'd make dinner just in case he comes home, and then Dave and I are going to a movie; master bought us tickets. I'd ask him if you could come along, but somehow I think he's not so happy with you just now."

"Yeah," Daniel said. "A movie? Really?"

Jane's smile grew wider. "Yep. Popcorn 'n' everything. Third movie we've seen this year."

And that, apparently, was all the conversation there was time for. It was already after five, and the master liked dinner at six. Jane handed Daniel his paper and banished him to the living room, where he sat reading in silence until Dave poked his head out of his bedroom and called teasingly, "Is it safe?" When Jane nodded, he plopped down on the couch near Daniel and flipped on some home improvement show.

Daniel really did want to get to know Dave better, but right now he wasn't feeling very social, and he was grateful Dave seemed to understand that.

The master walked in at 6:02 with a shopping bag in one hand. He went past Daniel without so much as a glance, but greeted Dave and Jane warmly. Still, Daniel detected strain beneath the smiles; the whole attitude was an act, just like yesterday.

"Got you guys something," the master said, passing his bag over to Jane.

Dave got up to join her, and Daniel looked on in wonder, surprised anew by the master's generosity. Not so surprised he'd been deliberately slighted, but definitely surprised that it hurt a little. He'd been very, very bad, after all. He deserved the master's scorn.

Jane reached into the bag and pulled out a bottle of wine. "For after the movie," the master said. "I made you two reservations down at the Terrace on 53rd and Madison, and it's BYOB. They know me; they'll let you in by yourselves."

"Oh, *thank you*, Master!" Jane threw her arms around his neck, stood on her tiptoes and planted a kiss on his cheek.

He looked a bit chagrined, but smiled and hugged her back. Dave just grinned and nodded. Daniel was starting to think he didn't talk much.

Jane disentangled from the master, looking as if she'd surprised even herself by her actions. "Dinner's waitin' now," she said, smoothing both hands down the front of her apron. "Come, sit down."

Daniel stood, but hovered between the couch and the counter, wondering if he should sit too. Jane had set two places—he'd shared every one of the master's meals so far, after all—but he suspected the man might be too busy pretending Daniel didn't exist to invite him to the table tonight.

The master confirmed that suspicion when he looked up at Jane and said, "Just one tonight." She frowned—right at the master, and he let her!—but cleared the second place setting without pause.

Well, Daniel wasn't really hungry anyway.

The master finished his meal and retired to his bedroom, wishing Jane and Dave a wonderful evening while ignoring Daniel like a world-class expert.

Jane approached Daniel after the master's door had closed, leaned down, and whispered, "Don't you mind him none." She gave his shoulder an affectionate squeeze and added, "Your supper's on the table. I'll be getting back late, so be a dear and wash your dishes for me. And remember, tomorrow you get to go back to work, and you'll both get a little space from each other; the master'll cool down and you'll unwind and everything'll work out just fine."

"Yeah." Daniel reached up to his shoulder to cover her hand with his. "I'm sure it will," he added, even though he'd been trained from his earliest years to never, ever lie.

Jane and Dave left soon after, leaving Daniel alone again but for the heavy press of the master's silent anger from down the hall. He could feel it even through the closed bedroom door, like a second presence in the room, stripping him of the pleasure of his solitude and the fine meal awaiting him. He pulled the middle from a piece of gluten-free garlic bread but tossed the crust, ate the tomatoes out of his salad but left the lettuce, and didn't even touch his lasagna. When he tried to finish the *Times*, it was as if his master were standing over his shoulder, glaring down his disapproval. Daniel gave up after reading the same sentence for the fifth time. He was afraid to turn the TV on lest he disturb the master with the noise. Not knowing what else to do, he sat on the carpet and tried some yoga, but he still hurt, and he couldn't shed his anxiety long enough to focus anyway.

Finally, though it was barely nine o'clock, he decided to call it an evening. He didn't think the master would bother him tonight, or want anything of him. He didn't even count on the master being willing to share his bed.

Still, orders were orders, so Daniel padded down the hall and sucked in a deep, steadying breath before entering the dragon's lair. Ready as he'd ever be, he reached out and turned the knob.

It was locked.

Fear swallowed his initial rush of relief. He'd thought he was in the shitter before, but this was bad. This was very, very bad.

Daniel backed away from the door, backed all the way down the hall, trying not to think of what might happen when the master finally decided to notice him again. Trying not to think of what would happen if the master told Tim or Mr. Foster how bad he'd been. He wondered if knocking on the door, dropping to his knees, and begging for the chance to pleasure the master would make a damn bit of difference. He wondered if the master would even let him.

No, he thought; the answer was probably no. And some deep part of him, the part that still clung to memories of Victor long after NewWorld had tried to beat them out of him, recoiled at the thought of giving up that one last intimate part of himself so easily, for so little, for *fear*. So he turned his back to the master's door, flipped out the lights with shaking fingers, and curled up on the couch, resigning himself to another cold and sleepless night.

CHAPTER THIRTEEN

Daniel awoke with the sun, stiff and groggy and unsure of where he was. Nothing new in that, though—when you traveled to disaster areas, war zones, and uncharted backwaters as much as he did, you got used to sleeping on foreign floors and waking up confused. Except he smelled coffee, which wasn't the sort of thing you'd expect in disaster areas, war zones, or uncharted backwaters . . . at which point he remembered he'd crashed on the master's couch because the man had locked him out of his room in a fit of justifiable anger.

And apparently, someone had draped a blanket over him.

He heard quiet talking, the sounds of breakfast being made. Dave must be getting ready for work. He rolled onto his back and full-body stretched, trying and failing to work the kinks out, then curled onto his other side facing the cushions.

"You awake, darling?" The soft question drifted in from the kitchen, quiet enough to ignore. And though he was still tired—positively wrecked, in fact—he mumbled out an honest reply. He closed his eyes, and next thing he knew, Jane was leaning over him.

"We're gonna be making some noise the next half hour or so. Why don't you go sleep in our bed where it's nice and quiet and comfortable."

Daniel rolled onto his back again and blinked up at her, completely unprepared for that offer. It seemed intrusive just to go into their room, let alone to lie in their bed where they lay together every night, where they talked and slept and made love. He didn't know how to respond.

Fortunately, Jane had it covered. "Come on now, darling; the sheets are clean, I just changed 'em. Up you go."

She peeled back the blanket she'd presumably covered him with earlier, took him by the arm, and pulled him from the couch. He shuffled along, passive and mute, let her deposit him into their freshly made bed. It was no less decadent than the master's, he noted with surprise. Just as large, covered in sheets just as fine and a down quilt just as thick. She pulled the bedding up to his chin and patted him on the chest.

"There now, isn't that better than the couch?"

Too sleepy to answer her clearly rhetorical question, he smiled and let his eyes drift shut. He heard Jane wind the blinds closed, but never heard her leave; he was asleep before she'd closed the door.

He woke up to her again sometime later, which cut down significantly on the strange-bed disorientation, though it still took a moment for things to slot into place. She was smiling patiently, holding a pile of folded clothes. "It's nine," she said.

Daniel frowned, wondering why the master had let him sleep so late, wondering if the next hour would be filled with last night's silent, jagged tension.

Jane, as if reading his mind, said, "Don't worry, darling, Master's off to work already." She put his clothes on the nightstand and slipped from the room, adding at the door, "I'm making breakfast."

Daniel mumbled a groggy thanks and followed her out, heading straight for the shower. As the hot water worked the couch-related kinks from his body, he realized, amazed, that he'd slept for over thirteen hours. He felt pretty damn good, though; even the cuts and bruises from the strapping only hurt if he leaned on them. Even better, he'd be back at work—his passion, his haven—in an hour, away from this place and focused on what he did best. Set to tasks about which there was no question, serving where his place was clear and valued. He rinsed off, shaved, dressed, and brushed his teeth quickly. He couldn't wait to get out of here.

But really, there was no point to rushing. His car wouldn't be here until ten. Still, he couldn't help himself. He slid into a chair at the kitchen table at exactly 9:20. Leg jiggling compulsively, he read the paper and ate ridiculously amazing homemade fruit crepes that made him wonder who had owned Jane before. The way she was feeding him, he'd have to spend some extra time in the gym burning off the calories, but that was just fine with him. He enjoyed the soothing, empty-minded focus of a long workout, the sense of effortless strength and the satisfying fatigue that followed, and Tim never begrudged him the time for it once the afternoon production meeting wrapped. Pain had kept him from those pleasures for four long days, and he was as eager to return to them as he was to the newsroom.

He greeted his driver warmly, smiled at the guard as he carded through the security gates at NewWorld, nodded cheerfully at two slave production assistants he passed in the hallway. He was still smiling as he strode across the newsroom floor, but his happiness faded as he approached his office and saw the door open, then disappeared altogether when he stepped inside and saw Tim, working at Daniel's desk and looking the kind of deadly serious that could only mean trouble.

Before he could even open his mouth to ask, Tim stood and said, "Mr. Foster wants you downstairs. Now."

Daniel's knees nearly unhinged, and he clutched at the doorjamb to steady himself. He couldn't . . . It was too soon after the last time, too—

"He didn't tell me why," Tim said, no doubt sensing Daniel's looming panic. "Maybe it's not . . ."

Except Tim didn't bother to finish that sentence, because there was *never* a happy reason for Mr. Foster to pull a slave from work. Which meant it had to be about his new master. The man must have called, complained. And didn't *that* just piss Daniel off, because if the master wanted him punished, he should have been man enough to do it himself. What kind of weak, weaselly, pathetic little man was Carl to do this, to *play* at master but shun the responsibilities of the title, to pass him off like some . . . some fucking unwanted *dog* he couldn't be bothered to train, let alone discipline, as if he was worried Daniel might try to bite back, or maybe just have the audacity to bleed when he struck him. The master obviously had no stomach for it, thought buying lives was some kind of game; or maybe he was just some bastion of bullshit left-wing liberal guilt who couldn't bear to do his own dirty work but had no questions of conscience when it happened out of sight.

Jesus *fuck*, he was furious.

Tim must have mistaken Daniel's rage-induced shaking for fear, because he came around the desk, cupped Daniel's biceps in a steadying grip, and said, "I'm sure it'll be okay. I'll come with you, okay? I won't leave you alone."

Daniel barked out a strained laugh that deepened the worry lines on Tim's face. At least *one* person in his life was willing to own up to who and what he was.

Anyway, maybe he was jumping to conclusions. Maybe Mr. Foster just wanted to talk, to warn him with words instead of the strap. Such mercy had been much more common under Mr. Krantz—especially for Daniel, for whom the man had had a soft spot from the day he'd bought him for NewWorld—but still, it wasn't unheard of now.

Daniel held on to that hope, and to his fury—it was easier to be angry than afraid—until they crossed the newsroom, and he saw Harper Bailey working at the guest desk near the hall. His knees failed and his mind blanked of all but terror at the sight; the guiding hand on his arm had to dig in to keep him upright.

They'd brought in a substitute. A fucking *substitute*.

Harper gave Daniel a knowing look—a wash of sick, distant sympathy—and turned back to his work.

CHAPTER FOURTEEN

"**B**reathe," Tim said, propping Daniel up against the elevator wall and pushing the *B1* button. Daniel thought that a remarkably wise suggestion, and even tried it for a while, but then he was breathing too fast and started feeling dizzy on top of everything else. So he went back to holding his breath, watching the indicator lights as the elevator descended.

Five. Four.

"I didn't know," Tim said.

Three. Daniel turned his head toward his handler but said nothing.

"About Harper. They didn't tell me they were bringing in a sub for the broadcast tonight. I would've told you. I didn't know."

Two. One. Daniel nodded once, silently absolving Tim of whatever guilt he was carrying. None of this was Tim's fault, and at least he had the guts to stand with Daniel when things got ugly.

The doors opened, and Tim had to physically remove Daniel from the back wall, where somehow, he seemed to have gotten stuck.

Daniel slowed as they neared the room where he usually went, but Tim pulled him past the door, shaking his head. Daniel couldn't tell if that was a good sign or a bad one, didn't know if there were other rooms down here with soundproof walls and whipping posts or if that was the only one. Didn't know if there were rooms even more sinister, rooms that held even darker fates.

God, he thought, a wan smile finding its way to his face, *you're getting downright melodramatic.*

Tim steered him into an over–air conditioned room four doors farther down, where Mr. Foster sat at a conference table, glaring as they walked in. Behind Mr. Foster stood two supervisors Daniel recognized from the edit bays. The room contained no whipping post, no chains that he could see; when he sank to his knees in front

of Mr. Foster, it was at least as much from jelly-legged relief as it was from training.

"Please," Mr. Foster said over Daniel's head—to Tim, Daniel assumed. "Sit."

Tim pulled a chair from the table and sat with the same look of loose-limbed relief that Daniel felt. But also like Daniel, his shoulders were tense; he was wary, waiting for the other shoe to drop.

"This isn't a friendly chat, Daniel," Mr. Foster snapped. "Take your clothes off."

Well, that shoe dropped awfully fast, didn't it?

He stood on shaky legs and stripped quickly, anxious to avoid agitating Mr. Foster further. Yet he saw no strap, no crop, no paddle. Only the shock prods on the supervisors' belts, which had no need of direct skin contact. Maybe Mr. Foster was just trying to throw him off-balance, embarrass and humiliate him. Or maybe he intended to set the supervisors on him with fists and feet, or to lock him down here, freezing and hungry and sleepless for days. Rarely did NewWorld damage their property like that, but they had brought in a sub, after all—clearly, they planned to incapacitate him.

He shuddered at the thought and sank back to his bare knees at Mr. Foster's feet. The floor was hard. He stared at a clean white line of grout in the groove between two tiles and wondered if Mr. Foster would make him bleed, if it would flow along the floor to stain cold, white squares in bright, hot red.

The toe of Mr. Foster's dress shoe butted into Daniel's stomach, less than a kick but more than a nudge.

"I suppose you're wondering what you're doing here," he said. Before Daniel could reply, the sole of that shoe slid down a few inches, pressed against his groin. "Think very carefully about the next words out of your mouth, Daniel."

Daniel hitched in a shuddering breath and said simply, "Yes, sir." He wasn't going to volunteer anything on the off chance he'd been called down for a different reason. Besides, he hadn't technically done anything wrong, and he was pretty sure Mr. Foster would hurt him no matter what he said.

The shoe dug in, and Daniel gasped, curled his hands into fists and willed himself not to flinch away.

"Let me try to put this into terms you'll understand, Daniel."

The condescension grated; he'd bet his freedom, if such a thing were even possible, that he was both smarter and better-educated than Mr. Foster could ever hope to be.

"A couple months ago," Mr. Foster said, "a Mr. Carl Whitman decided to lease a shiny new fuck toy. He shopped around, did his homework, compared hundreds, maybe even thousands of companions, and decided, for some unfathomable reason, on *you*. Maybe he just doesn't like dark meat, who knows. But imagine his surprise, his *disappointment*, when the expensive new toy he waited months to get his hands on showed up *defective*. It's like his toaster not making toast, or his DVD player not playing DVDs."

Mr. Foster shifted, leaned back in his chair, and stretched his legs; the foot pressing into Daniel's groin went from uncomfortable to sweat-inducing, but Daniel just clamped his jaw shut and took it like he knew he was supposed to.

"See, here's the thing, Daniel. He shouldn't have to *ask* his DVD player to play DVDs. He just jams one in there and hits play, and it fucking *entertains him*. It doesn't matter if his DVD player doesn't *want* to play DVDs. It doesn't matter if it would rather make toast, because that's not what it was bought to do, and good working appliances *always* do what they're bought to do. He shouldn't have to *ask* it to please play his goddamn movie. He shouldn't have to order it, or force it. He shouldn't have to feel like his fucking *appliance* is judging him, or resenting him, or hating him for expecting it to do what it's fucking meant to do! And he *certainly* shouldn't have to try pressing a million different buttons, or jiggling the remote, or whatever other *bullshit* you've put him through to get his fucking movie to play!"

The foot in Daniel's crotch jerked forward, punctuating Mr. Foster's point. Daniel hunched over with a grunt, then wrestled himself vertical again.

"So what does Mr. Whitman do? Why, he calls the store and says the merchandise is defective; he wants to return it."

What?

Another sharp kick in the crotch, and this time when Daniel hunched, panting and nauseous, he couldn't get back up. *Return* him? How had he not seen this coming? How had he gone on thinking he could slight the master over and over and still believe the man would keep him?

Easy: I didn't want *him to keep me.*

Mr. Foster grabbed him by the hair and yanked him upright, his foot still mashing Daniel's genitals. "So I say, look, I'll take care of it. Nothing wrong here that can't be fixed. Just a little programming glitch is all. And you know what he said? You want to know how unbelievably fucking *lucky* you are to be leased to a man like him? He said, 'Don't whip him, Eric. Not again.' He was quite insistent, in fact. Wouldn't agree to give you another chance until I agreed not to stripe your sorry ass."

He *what*? Daniel's eyes darted from the floor to Mr. Foster's face and back. The man looked disgusted, *pissed*. He shook Daniel by the hair and gave his nuts another little kick, as if he were personally offended by the master's imposition.

"What Mr. Whitman doesn't seem to understand is just how *above* it all you clearly think you are. How *spoiled*. How Mr. Look at Me I'm an Anchor thinks he's too fucking *good* to get down on his knees and suck some fucking cock! Well, I've got news for you, *slave*: I could sell your ass ten times a night down in Times fucking Square, and you'd suck it up like a good little boy and pretend you fucking love it. Because all this?" Another jab to his nuts that made Daniel's eyes water, made it hard for him to see Mr. Foster waving in a way that clearly encompassed Daniel's entire life. "All of *this* is at *my* pleasure, boy, you got that? And I will take it away and sell you each night like the fucking piece of meat you are if you do not"—*jab*—"get"—*jab*—"your fucking shit together"—*jab*—"right fucking now! *Do you understand me?*"

Daniel nodded frantically, unable to force even a simple *yes* around the pain bubbling up his throat. He believed Mr. Foster—believed every word. Oh, they wouldn't pull him off a successful broadcast, but that didn't mean they wouldn't pimp him out every night after the show. Plenty of famous slaves were put to that kind of work, and sometimes it was actually more lucrative for their owners than their day job. Hell, hadn't he seen a story over the wire just last month about some champion heavyweight slave boxer who'd raked in over a million at auction for a single postfight night of service?

Frankly, it was a miracle that NewWorld had waited as long as they had to lease out Daniel's ass. At least it'd only been to one man—one whose biggest kink seemed to be football, or possibly politics, or maybe just slaves with white skin. Daniel should've been *grateful*.

Probably would've been, if he were a better slave.

But clearly he wasn't, because . . . Well. Here he was.

Still, Mr. Foster drawled, "Good," perfectly civil again, his fury evaporating like so much smoke. "Good." He took his foot from Daniel's crotch at last—thank God—stood up, and smoothed his hands down the front of his shirt. "But just to be sure, what say we have a little practice session."

Just inches from Daniel's face, Mr. Foster unzipped his pants and pulled his half-hard cock out through the fly. "Go ahead," he said. "Beg me to suck my cock. Tell me you want it."

"Eric . . ."

Tim. Daniel had actually forgotten he was here, and his relief at the reminder was so powerful that every thought but one fled his mind: Tim would stop this, Tim would—

"I said beg me, slave."

"Come on, Eric, don't—"

"Damn it, Tim, I don't tell you how to do *your* job, do I? So kindly be quiet or wait outside."

Mr. Foster turned back to Daniel and slapped him hard across the side of the head. "Let's go, prettyboy. Convince me you want it. Convince me you'll behave."

He wanted to, *God*, he wanted to. He wanted to make Mr. Foster happy, he wanted to please his master, he wanted this basement hell to be over and done with, and yet he just . . . *couldn't*. If Mr. Foster were to grab Daniel's head, shove his dick down Daniel's throat . . . well then, fine, Daniel would take it, endure it. But to give away freely his desire—the one single thing that was his alone to control, that was tied so deeply to his memories of Victor, to love and attraction and happiness and pleasure—to taint those thoughts and feelings forever and pretend to *enjoy* it? No. He hadn't been able to do that for his master and he couldn't make himself do it now, either.

Maybe Mr. Foster was right; maybe he was too proud for his own go—

A shock prod jolt ripped the rest of that thought away, pain searing from his toes to the tips of his fucking hair. He screamed out his anger and his helplessness and his shame, and when the world came back, he was slumped between the two supervisors, still at Mr. Foster's feet, the business end of the shock prod still jammed warningly into his hip.

Mr. Foster grabbed his chin and jerked his head up. "Say it," he demanded, his cock brushing across Daniel's clenched lips.

Daniel could smell him—soap and musk and expensive cologne and the faint scent of wool. And he knew then, with a sad and terrifying clarity, that Mr. Foster would have to break him before he'd give this last little part of himself away.

Another mind-ripping jolt of pain, and for a moment, he hated himself almost as much as he hated Mr. Foster—for not rolling over, for not giving in to the inevitable without suffering so damn fucking much. Because it *was* inevitable, he knew that. NewWorld's will always was.

Mr. Foster squeezed his chin again, and the man's cock, fully erect, slapped against his cheek. "I said beg for it, Daniel."

Daniel tried. He thought the words, pictured them in his mind, imagined the feel of his lips and tongue shaping them. But when he opened his mouth, no sound came out. Only a whispered, "Please," a small, watery sound full of terror and regret. And then he was screaming again, screaming, and even through the agony of the prod he was aware of another pain, the supervisors' steel-trap grips on his arms, holding him in place so sickeningly tight that the bruises wouldn't fade for weeks.

"*God*," he choked out when it ended, half-stunned, half-praying, and then, "I'm sorry, I'm sorry," because really he was, and not just because it hurt so damn bad, even now, even after the last shock had faded.

Mr. Foster took a prod from a supervisor's hand and touched it to Daniel's cheek. Daniel whimpered and jerked—they weren't nearly as safe to use above the waist, surely he wouldn't—but he couldn't escape the touch. When the agony he was expecting didn't come, he released his sucked-in breath and said again, "Please . . ."

"You bring this on yourself, Daniel." And yes, all true, but knowing that didn't solve his problem. Mr. Foster ran the tip of the prod down Daniel's jaw, his neck, along the curve of his shoulder, down his side. "All you have to do is ask. Tell me you want me. Tell me you want to lick my dick like a fucking lollipop and I will stop"— *zap!*—"hurting you."

When Daniel stopped screaming this time, he was shaking, choking back tears, desperate to give Mr. Foster what he wanted, but still wholly unable to capitulate.

The prod dropped to his nuts and he closed his eyes in weary, horrified resignation, wondering just how stubborn he really would turn out to be.

Daniel was a deeply focused person, well accustomed to reducing his world to a single issue, a single set of facts, a solitary, quiet existence where a problem or puzzle drowned out all else for hours. This time pain swallowed his mind instead of logic, roaring noise instead of quiet—Mr. Foster's demands, his own screams, and the endless stream of desperate, teary words spilling from his lips: *please* and *I'm sorry* and *stop, God, stop*—but the focus was the same. That familiar, unbreakable intensity he was known for, or maybe cursed with. The prod went off again, and he thought, *God, what I wouldn't give to be someone else right now. Anyone* else. *Anyone at all.*

"Come on, Daniel," Mr. Foster snapped. "I'm not asking you to eat puppies or fuck your mother; all I want is for you to do what you were bought for. That's not so unreasonable, is it?"

Maybe it's not, he thought. Maybe *he* was the one being unreasonable.

"Sit him up."

He'd slumped over, ass beside his heels, chin to his chest. The supervisors hauled him back to his knees, fingers digging into pressure points in his biceps and armpits, and it *hurt,* fuck it hurt, and he wanted it—*needed* it—to end.

"Aren't you tired, Daniel?" Mr. Foster asked, eminently reasonable, his dick—long gone soft—still hanging out of his pants.

"Yes," Daniel whispered, because he had no voice left for proper speech, and because Mr. Foster had asked him a question and not answering would mean more pain.

"There's a nice, soft bed waiting for you back at your master's apartment, you know. You can have it, you can sleep the whole day if you want—but first you have to prove to me you deserve it. That you'll be a good little appliance and do what you're supposed to do. That this foolish, unwarranted *pride*"—Mr. Foster grabbed his chin again, jerked his head up—"that somehow seeped into your little slave head has disappeared and will not come back. Just a few simple words, Daniel. Tell me you want me."

"I . . ."

"That's it, Daniel." The hand on his chin slid to his cheek, his temple, stroked once through his sweat-damp hair. "You've almost got it."

"I . . . I want—"

I want out of here. I want the pain to end. I want never to lay eyes on you again. I want to hold on to the one tiny scrap of myself I have left.

Mr. Foster frowned, nodded at the supervisor with the prod, and Daniel wailed, "*Wait!* Please! Wait, don't! I . . ."

Mr. Foster was standing very, very close, his cock hardening as Daniel watched.

"Please," he choked out, but only just barely, the words like acid on his tongue. "I . . . I want you."

"You want me what?" Mr. Foster asked, his hand returning to Daniel's hair.

God, speaking those three words had been hard enough. Mr. Foster was going to force him into details? The hand in his hair tightened in warning, and even that little tug, that little pain, sent blistering shock waves through his overtaxed nerves. "I want . . . to suck your cock," Daniel said through clenched teeth.

"Say it like you mean it, slave."

"Please," Daniel managed to add.

Another nod to the supervisors, and for one terrifying moment, Daniel felt betrayed, cried, "No! I did what you wa—" But the men just let go of him, and he dropped hard to his hands and knees, panting with relief.

"Go ahead," Mr. Foster said. "Impress me."

Daniel reached up with shaking hands and placed them on Mr. Foster's hips. His muscles protested even that small motion after spending God knew how long clenched and spasming beneath the prod, and already there were stark red welts around his wrists, on his forearms, where the supervisors had held him. Too exhausted and uncoordinated to shuffle forward, he tugged gently on Mr. Foster's hips, inviting him closer.

"That's it." Mr. Foster stepped close. "Act like you want it. Say it again. Tell me you want to suck my cock."

"I want to suck your cock." The words came easier that time. In fact, Daniel was fairly certain he'd say anything at all that Mr. Foster asked him to. They were just words, after all. Just words.

He leaned in, closing the distance between them, and rubbed his mouth across Mr. Foster's erection. The man's scent this close was strong, but unpleasant only by association. He could do this. He *had* to do this. He parted his lips and wet them, touched them to the underside of Mr. Foster's cock, let his tongue brush the hot skin. It tasted like it smelled, soap and musk and a hint of salt, and when Mr. Foster breathed out, "That's it, Daniel, keep going." Daniel screwed his eyes shut and plunged, taking the entire head into his mouth.

Mr. Foster moaned and thrust forward, and it was frankly one of life's small miracles that Daniel didn't vomit all over him when Mr. Foster's cock bumped the back of his throat. Daniel reared back and quickly shifted one hand from Mr. Foster's hip to the base of his dick, leaving only a couple inches with which the man could thrust.

Daniel did his best to give proper attention to those couple inches. He even tried to look like he was enjoying it, though it seemed impossible to keep the revulsion off his face or hold in those little choking noises every time Mr. Foster dripped pre-cum onto his tongue. Not to mention he was so exhausted he could barely hold himself upright, let alone attend someone properly. And he really, really didn't like the way the supervisors were watching him, waiting, he supposed, for *their* turns.

Mr. Foster thwapped Daniel on the head and said, "My God. I think we finally found something you're bad at."

Daniel freed his mouth just long enough to say, "I'm sorry, sir; I haven't—"

"Yes, yes." Mr. Foster pushed Daniel's face into his crotch again. "I know. Practice will make perfect, no doubt. Besides, Mr. Whitman seems quite smitten with you. I'm sure he won't care how inept you are."

Daniel focused harder, though he didn't really know what he could do to improve. He'd not done this often, and though his small handful of partners had never minded his inexperience, Daniel liked to think he'd made up for it with enthusiasm. Now, however, he felt nothing but disgust—with Mr. Foster, and with himself for capitulating.

Mr. Foster sighed, yanked Daniel back by the hair. "Enough." And then to the supervisors, "Get him up."

They scooped him off the floor without a fight and threw him into the conference table hard enough to wind him, then spun him around and held him more or less vertical, ass propped against the varnished wood. He clung there, afraid of what they'd do to him if he fell, and realized with a slow, stunning sense of betrayal that Tim's seat was empty. The man had *left him here alone.* So much for having the guts to stand with him when things got bad.

But he didn't have the energy to be angry with Tim, didn't have the space in his brain to give it, not when he was so busy worrying about making it out of this room in one piece. He wanted to hope Mr. Foster was finished with him, but the man still had a raging hard-on, and Daniel didn't think he'd be leaving without taking care of that first.

"One more time, Daniel," Mr. Foster said, advancing a single step.

The supervisors' vise-grips on his biceps were back, and one had a prod shoved into Daniel's stomach.

"Tell me you want me."

"I want you," Daniel said, acutely aware of the implement of torture pressed to his middle. The words practically rolled off his tongue this time, less robotic than before. He even reached a hand out as far as the supervisor holding his arm would let him, showing Mr. Foster that he'd pick up where he left off if given the chance.

"Tell me you want me to fuck you."

"I want you to—" Daniel froze, body and voice, when he realized what he'd almost just said. What *Mr. Foster* had just said, and what he'd very clearly meant by it. "No," he whispered, too quiet to hear, but he knew the denial was etched into his face, into the tension of his aching body.

Agony then, and though he barely had the voice to scream anymore, he certainly tried. His body crumpled, but the supervisors kept him on his feet.

Mr. Foster tossed him a slightly peeved, slightly pitying, very bored look. "You don't get to *say* no, remember? We don't really have to go through all *this* again, do we, Daniel?"

Daniel sniffed back looming tears, wishing he knew how to give Mr. Foster the answer he wanted.

His silence was met with another shock.

"I do have other things to do today, you know."

Daniel barely heard him over his panting and the ringing in his ears, but the next words—"Beg me for it, tell me you're desperate to feel my cock up your ass"—cut deep through his fog of pain.

Mr. Foster barely gave him a breath's worth of time to reply before the supervisor shocked him again. The scream it ripped from his throat formed into a single word: "*Please.*"

"Please what?"

Daniel didn't think *please stop* would cut it, but he couldn't, *couldn't* go through that again. Not again. Besides, maybe being fucked wasn't really so bad once you were all grown up. His body was bigger now, could handle bigger things. Right? "Will it—?" Timidity and a cramp that ripped through his middle like another damn jolt cut him short. When the spasm ended, he tried again. "Will it hurt?"

Mr. Foster kicked Daniel's legs apart, took the prod, and pressed it firmly to the root of Daniel's cock. "Not *nearly* as much as this will," and *God*, Daniel didn't think it possible—when thought finally became possible again—that anything could ever hurt more than that.

"The longer you wait," Mr. Foster said, sliding the tip of the prod behind Daniel's cock, between his balls, "the more painful I'll make it. I could've made this nice for you if you'd just been a good little appliance right from the start and done as you were told."

Mr. Foster put the prod down and pressed himself flush to Daniel's sweaty body in a mockery of a hug, legs to legs and chest to chest. He was several inches taller, and his cock dug into Daniel's stomach like a hot steel pole. For a moment Daniel was eleven again, terrified and sobbing so hard he couldn't breathe, but the pain ripping through him was all too real, no mere memory, and it grounded him. He knew this wouldn't be pretty, but he also knew he wasn't walking out of here until he gave in, and at least it would be over quick.

"Now tell me you want me, Daniel," Mr. Foster murmured against his ear. "Buried balls deep in your ass. *Convince* me."

For one terrifying moment, Daniel feared he wouldn't be able to make the words come out, but then Mr. Foster stepped back and brought up the prod again, and Daniel blurted, "Please, I want you! Please!"

"You want me what?" Mr. Foster said, and Jesus, Daniel should have seen that coming by now, but it still somehow took him by surprise.

"I want you to fuck me," he mumbled, feeling his cheeks flush even through the strain of the last many minutes.

"You want to feel me buried balls deep in your ass."

"Yes."

"Say it, slave."

Daniel swallowed hard, lifted his gaze from the floor, and stared directly into Mr. Foster's eyes. "I want to feel you buried balls deep in my ass." *To end this. Anything to end this.*

"Let him go," Mr. Foster said to the supervisors. And then to Daniel, "Turn around, show me that pretty ass."

Daniel slumped over the table, laying his chest down flat and clutching hard to the edges. He knew he'd fall if he let go, not just to the floor but right down through it, spinning off into some terrible fucking nightmare from which he doubted he'd ever return.

Mr. Foster slapped him hard across the ass, more heat than pain compared to all he'd endured already; he barely flinched. He heard a condom wrapper tear, the squelch of lube. When a hand settled on each cheek and spread him wide, his fingers curled numb around the table and he whimpered once, soft and sharp, before he could stop it, remind himself that he was supposed to be pretending to like this.

"Say it again," Mr. Foster said, too many lube-slicked fingers shoving inside him, burning and stretching and scissoring. Daniel gasped, clenched his teeth. The pain coursing through the rest of his body did nothing to mask the new hurt, too full and jagged with awful memories and *shameful* somehow, raw nerves and the urge to squirm and push him out out out. "I said say it again," Mr. Foster growled. The fingers yanked free, and the blunt tip of his cock nudged at Daniel's hole. "All this trembling makes me not believe how much you want me."

"I want you," Daniel said, but he could not strip the frightened child's tone from his words.

Mr. Foster rammed forward, and Daniel screamed again, digging his teeth into the polished wood tabletop hard enough to make dents. Turned out it was no easier now than it had been as a child—agony, torture, like a strapping on the *inside*.

He didn't realize he was struggling, but he must have been, because the supervisors were grabbing his arms again, pinning his elbows and shoulders in pressure-point grips that made him beg in a long and desperate string.

Mr. Foster ignored it all, thrusting furiously behind him, driving him hard into the table edge with every ripping stroke, splitting him in two, in ten, in thousands.

God, how could Daniel ever bring himself to submit to this again?

As the minutes passed, that terrible, cleaving pain eased just a little, and Daniel lost both the strength and the will to keep struggling. When it was clear he'd no longer fight them, the supervisors released their punishing grips on his arms. One of them used his newly freed hands to rub his crotch through his pants. Daniel turned his head the other way and closed his eyes.

Mr. Foster never let up his frantic pace, his fingers digging into Daniel's hips with rough possession, yanking them back to meet each stroke.

At last he climaxed with a shout, pulled out abruptly, and pressed a hand between Daniel's shoulder blades to keep him in place.

"Look at me," Mr. Foster said, and Daniel realized the man had walked around the table, to the side Daniel was facing. He opened his eyes and saw Mr. Foster's crotch, half-hard dick and used condom and somehow, impossibly, only a few small smears of blood. "Now be a good little appliance and tell me how much you liked it. Tell me it felt great and you can't wait until I deign to fuck you again."

The words came out flat and scratchy-soft, but they came easy. After what he'd just given Mr. Foster, words were nothing. Meaningless.

Mr. Foster smiled. "Thank me."

That came out easy too. Dead. Toneless. But easy. Mr. Foster didn't seem to care. Daniel actually suspected he *looked* dead, slumped unmoving over a table, covered in welts and bright pink contact burns, too tired even to blink. He wanted to ask if he could go home, but home was his little cubbyhole on the top floor of the InfoGlobe dorm, and he knew he might never see that again.

"What do you think, gentlemen?" Mr. Foster asked as he cleaned himself with a wet wipe, and it actually took Daniel a moment to realize that he was talking to the supervisors and not to him. "You think he learned how to be a good little companion?"

"I think he was struggling an awful lot," one of them said. "Very unseemly."

"I think you're right." Mr. Foster's hand on Daniel's back pressed down harder. "All right, Daniel, let's try this again. This gentleman's name is Mr. Kreuner. Why don't you explain to him just how eager a cock-hungry little companion you are, and if you really, *really* enjoy yourself, then maybe you won't need to seek further satisfaction with Mr. Dalton here afterward."

Daniel's eyes closed in resignation, blinking away tears. "Please," he whispered to Mr. Kreuner, following orders and begging mercy all at once. "Please."

Mr. Kreuner bent down and licked Daniel's neck, and though all the words Mr. Foster wanted fell softly from Daniel's lips, he couldn't hear a single one of them over the screaming in his head.

CHAPTER FIFTEEN

aniel lay slumped on the floor beside the table, exactly where the men had dropped him, curled in on himself for protection and warmth and because he just couldn't seem to manage anything else. Mr. Foster had tossed a handful of wet wipe packets on him, and though he knew he was filthy, he hadn't been able to make himself take them. It seemed he had no control over his body at all—and wasn't that, he supposed, exactly what Mr. Foster had intended.

He was only alone for moments. Mr. Foster and the supervisors left, and seconds later, a frantic Tim came rushing in. He dropped to his knees beside Daniel with a startled exclamation, laid a hand on Daniel's shoulder.

Daniel didn't move, didn't flinch, didn't even bother to lift his head as he rasped, "Don't touch me."

"Jesus, Daniel, you—"

He hunched his shoulder in tighter, shaking off Tim's hand. "I said, *don't touch me.*" He hated the way the words came out, soft and weak from screaming, but Tim pulled his hand back anyway.

"You need help, Daniel. Let me h—"

"You left me," he spat, and he could see that his poison went straight to the heart. Tim flinched, hung his head.

"I had no power to stop him, and I didn't think you'd want me to watch them force—"

"You left me *alone* with them!" Daniel cried, shoving at the hand creeping back toward his shoulder. It was easier to be pissed than afraid, easier to be pissed than break down and cry. "How could you *do* that?"

The pain on Tim's face was stark and satisfying. Tim pulled his hand back again and whispered, "I'm sorry he did this to you, Daniel, and I'm sorry I didn't stay. I'm really . . . I'm *sorry.*"

Tim inched closer, and in his shock, Daniel let him; he literally could not remember the last time one freeman had apologized to him for the actions of another. Maybe years. Maybe never. "Please let me help you," Tim said—no, *begged*, and that was a first too.

He said nothing as Tim crawled around behind him, picked up a wet wipe, and ripped it open. It sounded exactly like the condom had when Mr. Foster had pulled it from its package. Daniel squeezed his eyes closed, held his breath.

"Shhh," Tim said, no doubt reacting to the tension in Daniel's body—the clenched muscles, the rapid breaths. "You know I'm not going to hurt you, Daniel."

People had been saying that a lot lately. Shame it never seemed to be true.

The wipe, cold and damp, came down on the back of Daniel's thigh. He twitched, then stilled. Tim kept up a steady stream of meaningless chatter—random words meant to soothe, to keep Daniel grounded—as he worked steadily toward the damage his colleagues had done. By the time a fresh wet wipe touched raw flesh, Daniel had almost, *almost* managed to unclench. The jolt of pain shocked him out of his stupor and he hissed, curled up his legs.

"Easy. I have to . . . I mean, I could take you to the infirmary instead, if you—"

"No." Daniel felt a blush creep up his face. He forced his legs apart again so Tim could work. "Please, don't." It was bad enough that Tim was seeing him like this, so raw and exposed, so roughly used; he couldn't bear the thought of a stranger looking at him, *touching* him, even though he knew he'd bled at least a little, could feel it dried on his balls, his ass cheeks. He wondered if he'd need stitches, how the fuck he was supposed to go to the bathroom for the next week, how the master—a man seemingly so kind and gentle—could ever possibly wish to do something so terrible to him not just once but every single day. He wondered how they expected him to function each night, to sit at his desk and read the news and interview guests and pretend he could still remember what it felt like to be happy.

"You know," Tim said on an uneasy laugh, "this is so not a part of my job description."

Daniel almost snapped, *Yeah, well being gang-raped isn't a part of mine, either*, but Tim sounded so helpless and uncomfortable that

Daniel didn't have the heart to make things any worse. Besides, he was just a slave, and slaves *couldn't* be raped, now could they.

"God, I'm sorry. I just . . . I don't even know what I'm saying. Just, just ignore me, okay?" Tim touched a wet wipe to rent flesh, and for a moment, the sting was so bad Daniel thought he would cry. It was absurd to fall to that, after all he'd been through today, and yet . . .

A hand smoothed up and down his spine, warm and gentle, trying to ease the hurt the other hand was causing. Daniel buried his face in his arms and held his breath. There was pain, sick and oily, hot and sharp like the shock prods. Then nothing.

"All set." Tim patted Daniel on the back of one trembling thigh before rising and offering him a hand. "It doesn't look too bad, after all. Can you stand?"

If you pull the right strings, he thought, a little hysterically, and took Tim's proffered hand. Between the two of them, he got vertical, but Tim had to prop him against the table to keep him that way. It took only a few hits with a shock prod to make your muscles weak and your nerves misfire for fifteen or twenty minutes; Daniel had *dozens* of little contact marks, tinged pink like sunburn, scattered all across his lower body.

"You know, maybe we should get you checked out after all," Tim said, eying him close. The man's gaze fell on half a dozen marks clustered just below Daniel's navel, slid to another cluster a few inches lower, then to the ones half-hidden by the thatch of reddish-blond pubic hair. Daniel hated the scrutiny, but he lacked the energy even to cover himself with his hands.

"I'm fine," he said, despite the sheer, mind-boggling absurdity of those words.

Tim, God bless him, nodded once and let the matter drop, turning his focus instead to getting Daniel dressed. Daniel slumped half against Tim, half against the table, barely able to work his arms through his sleeves by himself. Everything hurt in ways he'd long since forgotten were possible. He craved sleep like he craved air, and when Tim said, "Car's waiting to take you back to Carl's," he thought only of a house full of comfortable beds, of Jane and her painkilling salve, and of the master still at work for many, many hours to come. He simply would not allow himself to think beyond that.

Tim led him from the room, toward the elevator, supporting most of his weight as Daniel stumbled along.

"I asked them if you could stay awhile," Tim said as he hauled Daniel down the corridor, "but they claimed you'd be more comfortable in a bed than on your office couch. Frankly, I'd feel better if—"

If you weren't sending me off to be brutalized again?

"—if you were somewhere I could keep an eye on you. But they were quite insistent."

Daniel said nothing. He was too tired to walk and talk at the same time, and anyway his throat hurt, and he didn't know what he could possibly say. He wasn't willing to lie for the sake of Tim's feelings, not after Tim had left him alone, no matter how good the man's reasons.

The quiet of the elevator ride was short-lived, and then Tim was dragging him through the NewWorld lobby, toward a waiting car. The lobby wasn't crowded, but Daniel was still the subject of far too many stares: some curious, some pitying, some self-righteous or downright mean. Every single one of them felt like fingers on his skin, like hot breath and fresh bruises and blood. He shrugged out of Tim's supporting grip and made his feet go faster, stumbled through the front door, and nearly collapsed into the backseat of the sedan. Tim rushed behind him, hand outstretched, but his support was far too late to be of use.

"So, um," Tim began, hand on the car door, feet shuffling as Daniel fumbled with his seat belt. "You, uh . . ."

It wasn't like Tim to be lost for words. Daniel blinked at him, impatient, anxious to shower and sleep and uninterested in whatever platitudes Tim might try to offer.

But in the end, all Tim said was, "I'll see you tomorrow, okay?"

He closed the door before Daniel could reply.

CHAPTER SIXTEEN

Daniel fell asleep—or maybe passed out—on the short ride to the master's apartment. He woke up with a startled shout, huddled and cringing from the doorman's hand. Slaves weren't supposed to touch in public, but Daniel obviously needed help to stand.

The doorman was looking at him like he'd sprouted a third eye, probably wondering at the harshness of NewWorld Media, or maybe at Daniel's unexpected willfulness. After all, he'd needed help inside twice now in the short time he'd been here.

Daniel somehow made it off the elevator and down the hallway by himself, and Jane met him at the apartment door with thinly disguised panic and a helping hand.

"What happened?" she asked, ducking beneath his arm and pulling it over her shoulder, wrapping her free arm around his waist. "What are you doing home so early?"

She walked him to the couch and plunked him down—he was much too big and heavy for someone her size to support for long—then gave him a careful once-over. Daniel looked down to where her gaze lingered on his hands. Finger-shaped bruises had formed at his wrists and up his arms where the supervisors had pinned him, and his left pinkie was discolored and swollen, though he couldn't remember how that'd happened.

He blinked up at her, tired and mute. He didn't want her to know. He wanted to be alone, wasn't sure how to send her off without hurting her feelings.

"I need a shower," he said, though he hadn't meant to. Added, "I'm okay," and then, in direct contradiction and much to his embarrassment, "Help me up?"

She held out both hands, moving slow like she was worried he'd freak, and waited for him to take them. "That looks painful," she said, eying the darkening bruises circling his wrists when he locked his hands in hers. He nodded, but said nothing.

She helped him to his feet, steadied him when he nearly fell. "Prod?" she asked.

He nodded again, feeling his cheeks heat. If she knew that, what else might she—?

"Better use the bench, then. Don't want you slipping and banging your head." She smiled, a sad and gentle thing, painful to look at, and covered one of his hands with both of hers.

Whatever else she might have said then, she swallowed it when she met his eyes. He nodded once—gratitude for her silence—and let her prop him against her side and lead him to the guest bathroom.

He stripped without bothering to fold his clothes, stumbled into the shower, and curled up on the bench, staying there until the water ran cold. He lacked the energy for anything more than a perfunctory pass of soap over skin, barely enough to wash the stench of those three men away. His muscles were weak, twitchy and sore, locking on occasion into teeth-gritting cramps.

He shut off the water and stood, but his legs still felt disconnected from his brain, and he fell to his hands and knees. There he remained for far too long, gasping for breath and longing—for the first time since Victor—for the false security of his mother's arms.

But she's not here, and better for it. She shouldn't have to see you like this.

He grabbed the edge of the vanity and dragged himself to his feet. It seemed that Jane had collected his old clothes and left a clean cotton T-shirt and track pants in their place. He had to sit on the toilet to pull them on, but he was slowly regaining muscle control. The shower had helped.

His side cramped as he bent to put his sock on. He clutched at himself, hunched and panting until it passed, then finished dressing and headed back to the living room. He walked with one shoulder pressed to the wall, using it as a crutch until the hallway ended, then managed the last several feet on his own before collapsing onto the couch.

Jane appeared with a brownie and a mug of hot tea. "Eat; you need the energy." She smiled that same sad, soft smile. "And the tea will help your throat."

"Thanks." Daniel said, voice stripped to a scratchy whisper. He sipped at the tea, nibbled desultorily at his brownie.

Jane watched him for a moment, then sat down on the coffee table and turned her attention to her hands, clutched together in her lap. "I have two sons I've never met," she said.

Daniel's head jerked up, seeking her eyes. Her gaze was sad but steady; this was an old pain, long endured.

"My first master owned a culinary school in Georgia. I was born and raised on the campus. It was big; I barely even knew him. He didn't let his slaves teach officially, but I was handy in the kitchen, and the instructors liked me around. I was happy there."

She went silent for a long moment, but Daniel sensed this was not the time for him to speak. He broke off a piece of brownie and chewed it slowly, leaving no room in his mouth for questions.

"Master's wife was barren," Jane said. "They were both pushing forty. Wanted babies before they got too old, needed a mama who'd bear ones that'd pass. I was sixteen, one of only two white girls the school owned. Mistress picked me."

Another long silence, this one heavier than the last. Even in his addled state, it didn't escape Daniel what Jane was trusting him with. In most of the Western world, at least, children of a slave and a freeman were legally slaves, morally slaves. Also genetically slaves—or so prevailing scientific theory believed. If he told the wrong person, those kids' lives would be changed forever.

Jane reached for Daniel's plate and broke off a piece of brownie for herself. He offered her his tea to chase it down with, and she accepted with a nod. "Deal was he'd have me as much as he could handle during my most fertile week each month. But he wasn't never happy with just a week; his wife was over twice my age, and he couldn't do any old thing he pleased with her like he could with me. He wasn't a gentle man."

Brownie break number two. Daniel wasn't hungry anyway; he handed her his plate.

"I had a son when I was seventeen, another when I was nineteen. Never even laid eyes on 'em. Wet nurse came and cut the cord and took 'em away."

"I'm sorry," Daniel said, even though he'd meant to stay quiet, let her finish.

Jane shook her head. "I'm not. They don't know their mama's a slave. They'll never know what it's like to *be* a slave, if they live right. If they *can* live right, what with who their mama is." Her lips pinched together, and she dropped her gaze to her hands like maybe she was wondering what crimes and cruelties they were capable of, soulless as she was, as they were. "What more could a mother want?"

To see her children, Daniel thought. He had an older sister he could barely remember, sold away when he was three and she was seven. On the rare occasions his mother had spoken of her lost child, he'd felt her sorrow like a sickness, a wound never healed.

"Worked out good for me too, in the end. Mistress found the master stealing away with me long after the baby-making was done. Sold me off to one of my old students, who set me to cooking for his restaurant in the East Village. He was a good man, and I met my Dave there. And then Master Whitman got sick of paying to eat my cooking and bought us up."

She smiled again, patted Daniel on the knee, and pushed his plate back into his hands. "Finish your brownie, darling," she said, then stood to walk away.

"Jane?"

She stopped, looked back, kind and patient as ever. He wondered how she possibly could have known, though clearly she did. He wondered why he didn't mind that.

"You're probably wondering why I told you all that, eh?"

He was, but he thought it rude to say so, so he just shrugged.

"Because it gets easier. You get past it, and it gets easier. I wanted to make sure you knew that."

"I . . ." There was so much Daniel wanted to tell her: that he was honored she'd trusted him with her story, touched she'd relived her own pain to help him ease his own, grateful she'd understood his need more clearly than he'd understood it himself. But in the end, he simply said, "Thank you."

When she smiled at him, he knew that was enough.

"Get some rest, darling. You want to use our bed?"

The thought of that soft mattress and those smooth sheets was wonderfully appealing, but the thought of dragging his sorry ass the thirty-odd feet necessary to enjoy them was most definitely not. In the end, it wasn't worth it; the couch was comfortable enough. "No thanks," he said, sensing that Jane understood his reasoning.

He curled up on the couch, and Jane brought him a blanket. A vicious cramp seized his thigh as she covered him, and she gently peeled his hands away and massaged the muscle with a strength he'd never have guessed she possessed.

He supposed that was true of more than just her hands.

"I have some salve for the burns," she said, "and for the, uh . . ."

Well, wasn't that unlike Jane, to be flustered speechless?

"But I'm afraid I've got nothing to help with the cramps."

"S'okay," Daniel said. "I just need some sleep." Well, sleep was a good start, anyway. The cramps would fade with time, mellowing in an hour or two, disappearing altogether by morning. They were just damn miserable in the meantime, but it was better than before, better than—

Whoa. No going there. He was trembling bodily, clutching at the blanket like a shield, and Jane gave him that *look* again.

"Really," he said. "Just tired."

And then, as if to prove his point, he fell dead asleep.

The nightmares were bad, and he woke up with a jerk so hard he fell off the couch. He felt like he'd barely slept at all; a quick glance at the clock confirmed that it was just a little after four in the afternoon.

The apartment was silent and felt empty. *Running errands*, said a note on the coffee table. *Be back around 5. —J.* Beside the note was a chemical ice pack with its own note (*For your finger*), and her jar of salve. Daniel's legs seemed to be working again, so he took the jar into the bathroom and dabbed it over the contact burns he could reach, the blossoming bruises at his biceps and hips, forearms and wrists, the bite mark on his shoulder. The salve was cold, numbing relief on the surface, though pain still burned beneath. His hands shook when he glopped some on his fingers to smear on his ass, and he remained just levelheaded enough to marvel at Mr. Foster's power, at the man's capacity to make even Daniel's *own* touch revolting. That it hurt didn't help, but the salve worked fast, numbing the sharpest edges away.

He rummaged through the medicine cabinet with only the slightest shiver of apprehension at touching the master's things, came up with a roll of medical tape, and buddy-splinted his left pinkie to his left ring finger. It didn't seem misaligned, but it hurt enough to justify immobilizing. He'd have to get it looked at tomorrow.

With nothing else to distract himself from his thoughts or his exhaustion, he returned to the couch and conceded to sleep again.

Some hours later, he was back on the floor, lurched from a nightmare by his own scream. The sun was down and the room was dark, the clock not visible through the gloom. He smelled chicken cooking, or maybe turkey—strong and unappetizing in his current state—and heard soft sounds drifting through the closed door of the slave quarters. Dave and Jane, hopefully enjoying some downtime together. He was grateful she'd left him alone.

He crawled back onto the couch, retrieved the blanket from the floor and the remote from the coffee table. Though he knew it was illogical, downright absurd, he felt better stuffed into the corner, his back to the armrest and his knees to his chest. Even though there was nothing to hide from here.

Not yet, anyway.

He turned on the TV, skimming through the channels, not really processing what he was seeing. He settled on something colorful and bright, some Japanese cartoon that would probably induce seizures if you watched it too long, and muted the sound in deference to a budding headache. The show made for a lousy distraction; his mind kept turning back to this morning, to what would happen when the master came home this evening. To what he'd need to do if he didn't want to end up at Mr. Foster's feet again, begging for mercy that wouldn't come. Not even his anchor chair would save him if the master decided to return him for good. He couldn't let that happen.

He stared at the television screen, half watching the battling robots, half watching a whole different kind of violence playing in his head. He hugged his knees tighter to his chest and rested his chin atop them, pulled the blanket closer around his shoulders to ward off a core-deep chill.

CHAPTER SEVENTEEN

Daniel was jerked once more from sleep by a flash of light. He blinked against it, pressed the heels of his hands to his eyes, pulled them cautiously away. Not a flash; the room was still bright. Master's living room. Overhead lights. Someone had turned them on. Probably the same someone calling his name.

"Daniel!"

Shit. The master. His tone suggested he'd been repeating himself for some time already and wasn't at all happy about it. Daniel snapped from his stupor, unfolding quickly—too quickly, with a sharp hiss—to stand in his master's presence, but the man was already towering over him, both hands gripping Daniel's shoulders, holding him in place.

"What happened?" the master said. "Why aren't you at work?"

His voice was hard, stern. It had every right to be. Daniel had screwed up again, of course he had, or he wouldn't be here now. And of course the master would be angry; his expensive little appliance had done nothing but malfunction from the moment he'd brought it home.

No more, though. He couldn't afford to fuck up again, couldn't bear another correction at Mr. Foster's hand. Had no more pieces left unbroken anyway—gluing himself back together how the master wanted should be easy now. He'd convince the master to keep him no matter what it took. He'd make the master *happy*.

"I'm here to please you, Master," he said, passably convincing.

The master's hands tightened on his shoulders, and Daniel leaned in close, lifted fingers to the master's belt buckle and began to undo it.

"What are you—?" The master pushed his hands away. "Stop that. Wait. What are you doing? What happened?"

Daniel shook his head, brought his hands back up to his master's waist. He could see a bulge forming already in the man's pants, knew he was turning him on, so why was the master shoving him away? Fuck, couldn't he do *anything* right?

"I'm sorry, Master," he said, attacking the buckle again and again getting thwarted by the master's hands. He slid to his knees at the master's feet instead, pressed his cheek to the master's hip, his lips a hairsbreadth from the erection tenting the man's pants. "I'm sorry," he said again, "I—"

A hand touched his head, and though he dreaded the condescending intimacy of being petted like some child, some *creature*, he wished for it more than anything when instead the master's fingers came to rest on his forehead and pushed him back. If he were rebuffed . . .

"What the hell's gotten into you, Daniel? What are you—?"

"Please, Master. *Please*, I want to . . . let me make you feel good." Daniel rubbed his hands up the master's thighs, but he didn't dare touch the man's cock without permission. "It's just, you've been so kind to me, so generous all this time, and I've been so bad, so ungrateful for everything." Back to the belt now, and this time the master didn't stop him. He could feel the intensity of the master's stare on the top of his head, hear the master's quickening breaths, but whether from anger or arousal, he didn't know. Both, he thought—things were very bad, but he could still fix them if he tried hard enough. "I've taken advantage of your patience, and I'm so sorry, Master. I know I don't deserve another chance, but I—"

The master's huge hands caught Daniel's wrists, and Daniel gasped, pain sparking bright all the way past his elbows. His fumbling fingers stilled, their task unfinished; he'd been so nervous, so afraid, so *inept* that he hadn't even managed to pull the master's belt prong from its hole yet.

"I said *stop*," the master ordered, loud and slow, tugging on Daniel's wrists until he'd lifted him off his knees and dumped his sore ass back on the couch. "Just . . . just *stop*, and tell me what the hell is going o—"

This time, the master cut himself off. His eyes had locked with Daniel's, and whatever he'd seen there had silenced him midword. Daniel sniffed, blinked hard. His eyes were watering, and though he tried to convince himself it was pain, just pain, the stark truth was that he was terrified. The master didn't want him anymore. He couldn't even manage this one simple thing, and now he'd be sent back to Mr. Foster, to horrors he dared not even contemplate.

"What happened to your finger?" The master's voice had dropped low and dangerous, and with the hand still around Daniel's wrist, he pulled Daniel's arm forward to look at the taped-up pinkie.

"I don't know."

The master's face clouded over, as if he didn't believe him.

"Honest, Master," Daniel added, because Jesus, things were bad enough already, and the last thing he needed was for the master to think him a liar as well as incompetent and willful. It was getting harder and harder to blink the tears away, and even his voice shook as he added, "I really don't know, Master, I'm sorry."

The anger in the master's face radiated outward to his shoulders, his hands, and his fingers tightened on Daniel's battered wrists. Daniel clenched his teeth on a cry and closed his eyes against the master's fury, wondering how badly the man might hurt him before he threw him away.

His only hope was to distract him, to change his mind.

"Please," Daniel said again, and though he was begging full out, throat tight and burning as fiercely as his cheeks and ears, he didn't care, didn't care about anything but pleasing this man, about never seeing the basement of NewWorld Media again. He slid back to his knees, for though his hands were still not free, he had other tools with which to pleasure his master, as Mr. Foster had made so painfully clear.

But he'd just barely managed to press his open mouth to the master's cloth-covered, half-faded erection before he was jerked up and away again.

"No, damn it, stop!" The master hauled Daniel to his feet, and the hands that had been gripping his wrists moved to clutch at his upper arms, shaking him hard.

Daniel lowered his head so his master couldn't read the shame on his face, the humiliation or fear as he swiped at watering eyes with a trembling hand. "I'm sorry," he whispered, and then, "Please, Master, *please*," though even he didn't really know what he was asking for.

"What's this?" The master asked, deceptively gentle, tilting Daniel's chin up with one hand. Daniel could feel his face burning, his lips quivering, and when a single tear ran down his cheek, the master caught it with his thumb. "Stay," he said, taking his hand away and holding it before Daniel's face in a universal "don't move" gesture. "Just . . . just hold still for a second, okay?"

Daniel pressed his lips together and nodded. Would the master call his handler to come take him back now? Did he really think Daniel would try to run away while he went to get the phone?

But the master took only a single step back, his hands dropping to his sides, his eyes never leaving Daniel. They traveled slowly down Daniel's neck, shoulder, arm, widened in alarm at the bruises peeking out beneath Daniel's shirtsleeve, as if noticing them for the first time.

"Goddamn it," the master growled, reaching out to brush fingers over Daniel's forearm, the heavier bruising around his wrist. "What the fuck is this?"

Daniel swallowed hard and resisted the very strong urge to cover himself, to hide this new shame from the master's prying eyes. "I struggled, Master."

The master raised an eyebrow over a harsh scowl. "You *struggled*?" he demanded, as if he could hardly believe his recalcitrant slave would pile such an insult atop all the others that had led to his punishment in the first place.

"I'm sorry! I know I shouldn't have; I was weak, I didn't mean to misbehave again, I really di—"

"Damn it! He told me he wouldn't beat you! He promised!" The master turned his eyes to Daniel's, and if Daniel hadn't known better, he'd have said the man was downright beseeching. "I made him promise!"

Well, that was . . . different. So much so that Daniel had no idea how to respond. The truth, he supposed. "He, uh . . ." Daniel licked his lips, shook his head. "He didn't, Master."

No. What'd he'd done was much, much worse.

The master's scowl grew deeper. Perhaps he didn't believe Daniel, or perhaps he did and simply wanted to exact a punishment himself, for he crossed his arms and said, "Take your shirt off."

The master's voice quivered, much like Daniel's had these last many minutes, though surely the cause in the master's case was rage instead of fear. What was he planning? If he'd wanted sex, he wouldn't have stopped Daniel's earlier attentions. Which meant . . . *Oh God, please, no.* Daniel didn't think he could handle any more pain today. Not again.

Still, lest his punishment grow worse, he dared not keep the master waiting. He pulled his shirt over his head, wondering almost hysterically what the master's upper-crust neighbors would think of all the screaming coming from the north penthouse.

But the hands that fell upon Daniel's bare skin brought no pain. They were gentle, indecisive, tracing the bruises on his biceps, forearms, wrists, the smattering of contact burns on his stomach and chest, before spinning him around and repeating the process on his back. There were fewer marks there, but the master's fingers lingered long over the painful bite on Daniel's shoulder blade.

Those large hands turned Daniel around again, skimmed over his arms and chest like the hands of a blind man trying to map something unfathomably new. The touches burned with an intensity that infused the master's whole being—the master's hands trembled as Daniel shook beneath them; the master's breathing grew fast and audible as Daniel's own chest heaved with fear.

Maybe the master didn't want to hurt him after all. Or maybe he'd planned to, but had changed his mind once he'd been able to see and touch; maybe now, he simply wanted to take what he'd paid for. That'd be no less painful than a beating, but at least it wouldn't leave Daniel to contend with Mr. Foster's wrath again.

Daniel closed his eyes and tried to will the shakes away, forcing himself not to recoil from the master's touch. He even faked a quiet moan—no hard feat, since pain and fear and pleasure all sounded alike. But the instant the sound left his lips, the master's hands left his skin.

They returned a moment later, though, brushing over a long, thin bruise that ran hip to hip below his navel, where the edge of the table had bitten into him over and over with every one of Mr. Foster's and the supervisors' thrusts. Daniel dared a glance at the master's face, all creased eyebrows and pressed lips, but couldn't read what he saw there.

And then his eyes raced back to the master's hands when thumbs hooked in the waistband of his pants and underwear and tugged.

Daniel sucked in air like a beached fish, trying and failing to contain his rising panic. It'd be his own damn fault if he couldn't swallow it down; he knew the master wanted the illusion of a willing partner—an *eager* one, even—and Daniel was blowing his last chance to give him that.

No, not *was* blowing, *did* blow. The master's hands froze halfway down Daniel's hips, exposing a wide swath of skin but none of the parts that really mattered. Daniel swallowed back a sudden, vicious nausea, covered his face with shaking hands, and entertained, for a moment, the thought that it'd be okay to cry now.

After all, he had nothing left to lose.

Without a word, the master splayed his fingers across Daniel's bared hips, lining them up with one of the many sets of finger-shaped bruises that curved around from his ass to his pelvis. Daniel startled at the touch, reaching instinctively to push it away. He curled his hands into fists and forced them behind his back before they could commit such a grievous sin, but it was too late. The master's narrowed eyes traveled from Daniel's bared skin to his face and locked there. If before there had been a storm brewing in the man, now it was a tornado, a *tsunami*.

Daniel trembled in its wake.

Slowly, so slowly, the master's hands left Daniel's hips, settled his pants back into place, and then curled around his upper arms, applying pressure so slight that Daniel felt it only because he was exquisitely hyperaware. In this way, the master guided him back to the couch and deposited him there as if he were made of glass.

And then he spun around and kicked the coffee table—which *was* made of glass—hard enough to crack it.

"*Fuck!*" the master screamed.

Daniel wondered if it was because the master had just broken his furniture, or maybe his foot, or because he'd realized that Daniel had put out for NewWorld Media but not for him.

"God fucking *damn it!*" The master grabbed the television remote and hurled it into the wall, where it shattered into a spray of plastic bits and batteries. Another shouted string of profanities, and the master reached for the cushions on the empty couch, flung them toward the hall, the kitchen, the window. Daniel huddled into himself, brought his arms up to his head, yet his gaze remained pinned on the storm raging through the living room.

"*Shit!*" The master upended the now-cushionless couch, then kicked the underside hard enough to punch his foot through the fabric. He wrenched it out with another furious shout, stomped around the couch, and cleared the nearby kitchen countertop with a long and livid arm swipe. A basket of fruit splotched to the floor, a notepad, a knife block. The master scooped it up, and Daniel whimpered "I'm sorry!" just in case the man planned to start throwing the knives.

God, what had he done to cause this? Such fury over nothing made less sense than the master trashing his apartment instead of his slave.

The master hurled the whole knife block into the fridge hard enough to dent the appliance door, and Daniel cried "I'm sorry!" again.

The master froze. Then his head whipped around, and Daniel reflected for an instant on how absurd this would all seem if he weren't so goddamn fucking *frightened*: the master was standing one foot in front of the other, his right arm drawn back behind his ear, his fist clutching a banana so hard the fruit was oozing through the burst seams of its skin. Like a baseball player, or a monkey, winding up for the pitch.

"What?" the master asked, sharp and breathless.

Daniel cringed, but forced his voice steady. Well, steady enough, anyway. "I said I'm sorry, Master. Whatever I did wrong, I'm sorry."

The master's face went slack as suddenly as if he'd had a stroke. The oozing banana slipped from his fingers. He crossed the floor in three huge strides, dropped to his knees beside Daniel, and threw strong arms around Daniel's huddled shoulders. When Daniel stiffened, the master pulled him closer and whispered, "Shhh, no, no, Daniel, it's not you. Not you, I'm not mad at you, I swear."

. . . What?

One of the master's arms unwrapped just far enough to snake up to Daniel's head, stroke through his hair. "I'm sorry, I didn't mean to scare you. I'm so sorry."

What?

Surely he was imagining the master's words. Hallucinating, cracking under the stress. But the master kept repeating himself, over and over, interspersing apologies and assurances with stroking hands and a soft press of lips to Daniel's forehead, cheek, the top of his head, the side of his neck. "It's not you." *Kiss.* "I'm sorry I scared you." *Kiss.* "I'm not mad at you, I promise." *Kiss.* "You've done nothing wrong." *Kiss.* And on and on and on.

Gradually, Daniel's shaking subsided, and he relaxed into the master's arms as the true import of the man's words sank in: If the master wasn't mad at *him*, then that left only those who had hurt him, only Mr. Foster and the supervisors and NewWorld Media. Which meant the master wasn't going to punish him, wasn't going to return him, certainly wasn't going to tattle to Mr. Foster on him. Hadn't even meant for any of this to happen.

And as slowly as that realization had dawned upon him, a new one began to take root in the fertile ground his terror had left behind.

Anger.

He was *angry*. What the fuck *had* the master meant to happen, if not this? What had he possibly thought could come of telling Mr. Foster he'd been obstinate and useless? The master wasn't a stupid man; how could he have been so stupid about *this*? About Daniel's safety, Daniel's *life*?

The master's arms tightened again, not hurting but clearly not letting go anytime soon. He placed a fluttering kiss on the shell of Daniel's ear and said, voice tight and shaking, "I had no idea he would hurt you. You just seemed so unhappy, and we never got along like I thought we would and I didn't want to force you to stay here if you were miserable, and . . . and I'm *so sorry*, but I swear to you, I will *never* let anyone hurt you like that again." *Kiss.* "I promise, do you understand?" *Kiss.* "*Never.*"

Another kiss to his ear, his temple, his cheek, and Daniel couldn't stand it anymore; if he didn't get this poison out, it'd kill him, and it'd kill him ugly. Worse even than this afternoon. The master came in for another kiss, and Daniel hunched away from it, threw both hands up and actually *kept* them there, even as the master's chest bumped his palms.

"Wait," he said, "please," even though what he *really* wanted to say was *Fuck right off and fuck you*.

The master backed off instantly, and that single gesture—a legal and ethical expectation among freemen but a courtesy and consideration a slave could never, ever expect—took Daniel's fire right along with it. The anger dimmed, and he lost the courage to confront the master, even when he said, voice full of care and concern, "What is it, Daniel? Talk to me."

Daniel shook his head, frustration burning his eyes and throat. He didn't want to cry in front of this man. Especially not when the worst was already over.

Or so he hoped, anyway.

"It's okay, Daniel." The master brushed fingertips under Daniel's left eye, which was stinging with tears. "It's okay. I mean it, no one's *ever* going to hurt you like this again, least of all me. You understand?"

"Yes, Master," he said, breathless, voice shaking. He wanted desperately to believe it, but he'd learned long ago that nothing was ever so simple, so easy, given so freely. Besides . . . "You won't . . . I mean, don't you want me to—?" He couldn't finish, afraid that saying it might somehow summon it, remind the master of why he'd bought him. Yet at the same time, he had to know.

The master coughed up a noise that might have been a laugh, pressed another kiss to the top of Daniel's head and rubbed his hands up and down Daniel's back. "Of course I *want* you, Daniel. I've wanted you for years. But it's *you*, Daniel—your mind, your experiences, your sense of humor, your passion for the work we do, your bravery and your determination and your stubbornness. We even live in the same damn fishbowl, Daniel; *that's* what I wanted to share with you. I wanted a *friend*. Someone who understands this life we live. It was never just about sex, and I'd *never* force you or hurt you. It doesn't have to be . . ." He paused, puffed a hard sigh against Daniel's hair. "It's supposed to be *good*, Daniel, it's supposed to make you feel good. Whoever did this to you . . . They were cruel. They were *bastards*. It's not supposed to be like that; I wouldn't ever make it be like that, I promise."

Another kiss to the crown of his head, and Daniel turned his face up to study the master's openly, to look into his eyes and read the truth he saw there. The fierce conviction.

This man meant every word he'd said.

And in an instant, Daniel was furious again. They didn't share *shit*, and how dare he presume to think so, to be so certain that just because *he* wanted Daniel, Daniel should want him in return? How dare he claim to want Daniel's stubbornness and determination, yet try to return him when he got it?

The *master*, dense as ever, seemed not to notice Daniel's fury. Just kissed him on the forehead and said, "I will *never, ever* hurt you, this way or any other. Do you understand me?"

"But you *did*," he blurted, and the master looked just as horrified as Daniel felt at what he'd let come out of his mouth.

The master slowly rose from his squat at Daniel's feet, sat down on the couch next to him, never taking his eyes off Daniel the whole time. If he meant it, if he meant what he'd just said about never hurting Daniel, then talk would come next rather than discipline. But the day had been too long and entirely too bleak for Daniel to get his hopes up.

Until the master turned sideways on the couch to meet Daniel's eyes, took Daniel's hand in his, and said, "You're right. And I'm sorry." The master's eyes were watering, his lips pressed flat and unhappy. His gaze darted down to their joined hands, lingered a moment at the bruises on Daniel's wrists, then crawled slowly back up to Daniel's eyes. "This is *my* fault. All of this. I was careless and I didn't think and I got you hurt, and I can never apologize enough for what happened to you today because of me. But I hope that maybe one day you'll be able to forgive me, and in the meanwhile, I'm going to do everything I can to regain— No, because I never earned it in the first place, did I? I'm going to do everything I can to *earn* your trust, Daniel."

Daniel blinked at the master for he didn't even know how long, brow furrowed, lip curled in confusion. His hand in the master's was sweaty, shaking, and if brains could sweat and shake too, his would be doing both right now. He couldn't . . . he didn't *understand*. "I . . . Are you saying . . ." He shook his head, shook it again. The anger had poofed away, and he wanted it back because it was so much easier than *this*, whatever this was. So much *clearer*. "I was a bad slave," he said slowly, testing these strange new waters. "I was *terrible* to you. Ungrateful. Willful. Obstinate."

But the master was shaking his head before Daniel could even finish. "No," he said. "*No. I* was a bad master. Do you realize . . . I mean, we've never really *talked*, you know? I should've told you myself how

I was feeling, what I wanted. I should've been clearer. And I should've known..." His free hand squeezed Daniel's knee, chaste and urgent. "I should've known that Eric would be so damn *literal* about his promise. I was a fucking moron, and I would've never said a word to him if I'd realized, Daniel. I *wouldn't* have. I don't want to send you away, and even if I did, I'd *never* have knowingly sent you back to..." He tossed his hand up, horror stamped clear across his face. "To *that.*"

"You won't do it again?" Daniel asked, outrageous as it was to question the master like that, but the man was clearly in a repentant mood and Daniel needed to know. Needed to hear it direct from the master's mouth, because the man *had* been an idiot. Criminally so, if he really hadn't understood the way his actions would have consequences. Daniel's head was spinning with the implications of the last few minutes, with the way the master was looking at *him*, begging *him* for understanding and forgiveness, with the power and the strangeness of that. But it wasn't enough, not quite. Before he could truly hope to trust the man again, he needed the promise.

"No, Daniel. I won't." He squeezed Daniel's hands, and when he blinked, the moisture in his eyes spilled over, one tear down each cheek. "I swear I won't. I'm so sorry. I'll do better. I swear."

Daniel sniffed back his own tears. This time, he really did believe the master, his relief so profound that for a moment he couldn't even name it, couldn't identify the release of the tension he'd been carrying for so long, the panic and the helplessness and the fear. Only after the tears came again and he didn't bother to stop them did he understand: he'd endured a terrible thing, but it was over now, it was *over*, and there were strong arms around him and the safety of a man who cared, who wanted to protect him, who'd *sworn* to protect him and was strong enough to say he was sorry and take responsibility and shelter him, like no one had since Victor, since his mother, and he wept into his master's shoulder without shame and soaked in the comfort the man offered.

The master pressed his face into Daniel's hair and breathed deep, stroked hands up and down his arms, his back, held him tight and peppered his head with kisses. Daniel tilted his wet face back and let those kisses fall on his forehead, his nose, his chin, took a deep breath and let the next one fall across his lips. Thanking the man the best way he knew how, and not minding it after all.

The master froze, panting slightly, soft breaths puffing across Daniel's mouth, and with the utmost care he placed another small, dry kiss upon Daniel's lips. He asked for nothing more, took nothing more. It didn't feel like being used, Daniel thought. It felt, shockingly enough, like being loved.

CHAPTER EIGHTEEN

Daniel awoke as he'd fallen asleep: cocooned in his master's arms, snug against a warm chest, two pillows, and three blankets. He hurt everywhere—except, he realized, the one place that mattered most.

He wasn't afraid.

"Are you okay?" the master murmured into the back of his head.

The fear returned in a flash; had he done something to wake the man? The sun had barely risen, he'd be angry—

"Daniel?"

No, not angry. Daniel's heart calmed, and he chided himself for succumbing to instinct. He wasn't an animal; he didn't have to let it rule him.

"Yes, Master," he said. It might even have been the truth.

"Good." The master kissed the back of his head again. "But I'm calling us out sick today anyway."

Daniel hadn't even finished taking a breath for his protest before the master added, "Don't bother. There's no arguing with me about this."

God only knew why he'd thought to argue, anyway. If the master said he needed the time, not even Mr. Foster could fault him for it. Besides, he hurt to the point of distraction, would surely be useless at work. All he wanted to do was sleep.

Which apparently he did, because next he awoke, the sun was streaming bright through the blinds in the master's bedroom, and the master and another man—no, a slave; he was black—were standing over him, talking softly.

He drew the blankets tighter around his shoulders and waited for someone to tell him how to react.

"This man's a nurse practitioner," the master said. "He's going to look you over, okay?"

Daniel nodded, wondering why the master had even bothered to ask.

He had to strip again, even his underwear, so the NP could examine him. But the master held his hand, and Daniel clutched it without shame, those strong fingers squeezing out the worst of his fear.

The next minutes went by in a strangely dichotomous haze of pain and numbness, Daniel staring resolutely at the loose button on the NP's shirt—he should fix that; the man's owner would be upset if it fell off—doing as the NP asked and moving where the NP put him. The master kept a hold of his hand throughout, radiating concern, looking like he wanted to help but not knowing how. Daniel wished he had the words to explain just how much the man was helping already.

When the examination ended, the NP gave him a shot. "Antibiotics," he said. "I'll be back tomorrow," he said. Whatever he said after that was lost to a metallic taste in the back of Daniel's throat and the panicked realization, brief though it was in his last few conscious moments, that the NP had put him to sleep.

Not sleep, the master told him when Daniel woke again, half-surprised that he had at all. Just a painkiller. Daniel thought the drug might still be working, for he sat up with only minor complaints from his body. His trip to the bathroom, however, was torture, like shitting broken glass, or maybe a porcupine. His face was wet when it was over, his lip sore from where he'd bitten it. The master steered him back to bed with soft words and softer hands, laid him on his back, and brushed a kiss across his forehead.

"Do you trust me?" the master whispered.

"Yes," Daniel said, surprising even himself. Words were cheap, after all, and the master had been so careless; maybe he was foolish to trust him now, but there was no changing how he felt.

"I want to make you forget your pain. Will you let me?"

"Yes," he heard himself say again.

Another brush of the master's lips against his forehead, his jaw, then his own lips, tentative and tender. Daniel opened his mouth just a little, felt the master's mouth curl soft and sweet around his lower lip. There the master lingered, sharing skin and breath, and it was fine, okay, nothing like what those men had done to him the other day. Maybe too much, though, like what he'd shared with people he'd actually loved, or at least desired of his own accord, and his breathing sped up as his heart beat faster, nerves and nausea creeping in. But he held still as the master's hands crept beneath the hem of Daniel's shirt, shivered across his belly and flanks, then paused as if seeking—*surely not?*—Daniel's permission.

Except, yes, that was *exactly* what the master wanted. "Tell me if you want me to stop," he murmured against Daniel's lips, and though his instinct was to lie here, to let the master do what he so clearly wanted, he decided to take the risk, to *trust* the man like he'd said he did.

He sucked in a breath and closed his eyes and prayed to whatever powers might give a shit about his life, and then said, "I'm sorry, Master. Please. Stop."

The master's lips and hands left his skin, and no retribution came, only a soft, "Okay." A pause while the master settled beneath the covers, body close but not touching. While Daniel's breathing returned to normal and his mind slowly wrapped around the idea that the master had not only asked for but actually *respected* his wishes. That what he'd wanted mattered. More, even, than what the master wanted.

He was still marveling at that when the master said, "So I'm starting to think Nathaniel Bishops is right."

Daniel rolled his head to the side to meet the master's steady gaze. "About what, Master?"

The master shrugged. "Everything, more or less." He smiled gently, though his eyes looked troubled, and touched fingertips to Daniel's forearm. "You're a lousy slave, you know."

Daniel's pulse picked back up at that, but the master's smile and touch both remained so gentle, he couldn't have meant it in anger.

"I'm just saying, nobody's found the gene yet. What if it's like eye color instead of sex? Two brown-eyed parents *can* pop out a blue-eyed kid. One time out of four, in fact, if they're both recessive carriers. Even if we assume only one out of every ten or twenty are recessive carriers, that's still . . ." His face scrunched up, and Daniel waited in the silence, breath held and stomach twisting, to see where this would go. "Well, I'm bad at math, but it's still *some* kids, sometimes, however rare, born without the slave gene, even if they come from two slave parents."

Another silence. Except this time the master clearly wasn't doing math in his head. He was staring right at Daniel, waiting for him to speak.

"I'm not doing a story on this, Daniel. I just . . ." The fingertips on Daniel's arm brushed once, hesitantly, back and forth. "I don't want to make any more mistakes, you feel me?"

Oh yes, he felt him, all right. He knew *exactly* how that fear felt—more, he was certain, than the master ever could. And yet . . . the man was opening up to him in a way that seemed unprecedented between master and slave. And he held so much power over Daniel's life. If Daniel could convince him to use that power to make it better . . . "Are you saying you think I don't have the gene, Master?"

The master shrugged, folded his arms behind his head and blinked up at the ceiling. "I guess I'm wondering if all those functional MRI results in support of the gene are because slaves really do inherently lack emotional response and empathy, or because the lives in which they were raised dampened those feelings by necessity, by nurture."

"Or because we have no souls?" Daniel ventured. This was dangerous ground, all of it, but he'd spent his whole adult life facing down dangerous ground. Besides, he was pretty sure Carl Whitman wasn't a church-on-Sunday kind of man, that he'd somehow climbed the ladder despite that.

But the master just shrugged. Said, finally, "I don't know. Maybe there are no souls, not in anyone." A pause, and then, "Maybe nobody's been able to find the slave gene yet because it doesn't actually exist."

Daniel nearly left things there, but in this bubble of newfound trust, this sense—false though it might turn out to be—of real safety, he couldn't help but risk one last step onto unsteady earth. "Yet you own slaves."

The master nodded. "I do." Another long pause, but still Daniel felt no fear of it. "Maybe I shouldn't." And again, a silence that invited Daniel to fill it.

He felt less fear this time, speaking up. "Do you know any free black people at all?"

The master was surprised by this turn of conversation, if his climbing eyebrows were any indication. "In America? No, not one. I'm not even sure there are any; who'd want to live in a place where everyone just assumes you're a slave?"

Daniel nodded. "You know what NewWorld taught us in school about black people? That the *entire race* is inferior. That they *all* carry the slave gene. And that the chronic poverty, warfare, and disease on the African continent is the natural consequence of whole nations full of slaves without masters, which is why we should all be so *grateful* that we have NewWorld to look after us."

"They taught us the same thing, to be honest."

"But I've *been* to Africa. More than once. Nigeria, Sudan, the Congo, Ethiopia, Kenya, Uganda, Niger, Zimbabwe, Somalia, and on and on. And I've met plenty of good freemen there, bright freemen, hardworking freemen. Those people are *suffering*, and it has a lot more to do with their old imperial masters drawing random lines on the map and stripping the continent of its resources than it has to do with soullessness. America did it four hundred years ago when the Red Death killed off so many colonists and Europeans that shipping those 'soulless savages' from Africa started making economic sense. The first generations of African slaves in the US? The vast majority of them hadn't done *anything* wrong. They weren't criminals, they weren't debtors, they weren't children of slaves. They were freemen just like you, and they were stolen right out of their homes and put in chains and shipped to a lifetime of servitude because they *looked* different, because they worshipped different gods, and nowadays everyone just seems to conveniently *forget* how the ancestral origins of every last one of the thirty million black slaves in this country completely fail to align with every last one of the supporting causes for the institution. And not only do they forget, but they're *still doing it now*. Abducting freemen out of Africa may be against the law these days, but nothing stops you from as good as enslaving them there in the local diamond or rare earth metal mines, or arming and riling up warring factions to serve your political needs."

Daniel didn't even notice what a lather he'd worked himself into until he realized he'd sat up and was looking down at the master's open-mouthed, tight-eyed expression.

Shit. He'd gone too far. Done exactly what Mr. Foster had so recently and painfully warned him against: forgotten his fucking *place.* "I'm sor—"

The master held a hand up to silence him, and Daniel closed his mouth so hard his teeth clacked together. "They don't teach us *that* in school," the master said. Then the lines smoothed out of his forehead and his parted lips curved into a gentle smile. "Please, go on. I want to hear more. What else don't they teach us?"

Huh. That . . . wasn't the reply Daniel had been expecting. But he saw no trace of mockery or anger or derision on the master's face, so what the hell. He was wary to speak again, knowing how easily he'd just forgotten himself, but that particular horse was already so far out the barn door it'd galloped clear across the country. If the master meant to trap him, he had more than enough ammo by now. So he replied, "That your justification for killing or enslaving every last Native American in existence is just as flimsy as your justification for black slavery."

The master raised an eyebrow, but still he seemed only curious, not affronted. "Oh?"

Daniel nodded, leaned back against the headboard and stared at himself in the mirror on the opposite wall. Watched the blasphemous words falling out of his mouth. Watched the *passion* on his face, the confidence, the surety, and hardly recognized himself. "Sure, yes, they spread the Red Death to the colonists, and the colonists spread it to Europe, and it wiped out nearly half the empire. But it's not like they did it on purpose, and if that's a message from God, proof from on high that the natives were soulless savages and heartless killers, then what about us? *We* gave them smallpox, and we *did* do it on purpose. You know how hard it is to find a history book that's willing to mention the fact that our disease killed over eighty percent of *their* empire? Yet we were the ones with the guns. Ergo, we had the moral high ground."

That felt somehow like more of an overstep than the last thread of this discussion—*no, not discussion,* lecture—so Daniel forced himself quiet again, stole a glance at the master's thoughtful face and waited for him to say something.

What he finally *did* say was almost . . . disappointing: "Hmm."

That was it? *Hmm?*

After perhaps a minute of silence, the master followed that up with, "So what about now? There hasn't been a free black or native in this country in centuries. Even if we magically decided we've been wrong all this time, there's close to forty million slaves here between the two races. You can't just *release* them; they don't know *how* to be free. And what about everyone else? The white slaves? The Asians? The Hispanics? The ones whose ancestors were conscripted for valid reasons? And even assuming the blacks and natives were unfairly conscripted all those centuries ago . . . if nearly every other race and country in the world has a fifteen to twenty percent slave population, then surely at least fifteen to twenty percent of the blacks and natives were legitimately born slaves too?"

Daniel shrugged; it felt a lot safer and easier to argue his position when the master wasn't arguing back. "I guess," he said.

The master scowled. Did he dislike Daniel's answer or the return of Daniel's timidity? "Okay. So, maybe Dave should never have been a slave. But rightly or wrongly, he still is one. The law says they have to be owned by *someone.* Best someone who's good to them, right?"

"Right," Daniel agreed, because that much was definitely true. It didn't explain the master leasing him, though. "I already have an owner, and yet you paid for me."

Another shrug. "I was weak." The master rolled his head to meet Daniel's eyes. "Still am. Besides, your owner isn't good to you."

Not that the master could've known that before he'd leased Daniel. Not that *Daniel* had known that before the master had leased him. But looking at how the master treated Dave and Jane, he had to admit he saw some truth to it now. "Things are what they are," he said, because even now, with this new trust between them, with all he'd said about the problematic history of slavery in this country, he'd be foolish to speak a single bad word about NewWorld.

The master nodded, covered one of Daniel's hands with his own. "Yeah. But maybe they never should've been, and maybe they don't always have to be. Maybe things can change."

Daniel's fingers clenched around the master's, and for a too-long moment, despite all the remarkable things they'd just said to each other, he simply couldn't *breathe*.

But he forced his lungs to start again. He didn't want to think too closely about what the master had just said. It was bad enough he was really starting to like the man—they weren't friends, couldn't ever *be* friends, and forgetting that was even more dangerous than everything else he'd said tonight. Adding some ridiculous hope for a free future to the mix would only screw up the present. So when the master's fingers gave his own a gentle squeeze, and the master's open, patient expression quietly asked, *What do you think?* Daniel said simply, "I'm tired, Master." Which in itself was a test of hope: Would the master care? Be angry? Let Daniel's needs matter again like he'd seemed to let Daniel's thoughts and opinions matter so much this evening?

The master's expression wilted—a moment's disappointment, maybe even a flicker of anger—but then he smiled a soft gentle smile and touched Daniel's cheek with his fingertips and said, "Yeah, okay. Get some rest, Daniel. We'll talk again later."

Strange, but Daniel found himself looking forward to it.

CHAPTER NINETEEN

The master called him out of work for the next two days. He didn't need it, not really, but he was grateful for it. The awkwardness between them had evaporated sometime between the master destroying his living room and discussing manumission like a possibility worth fighting for. Daniel wasn't even worried about NewWorld—a sub for a couple days cost an awful lot less than the master's six mil they were worried about keeping, and the master keeping him home was as good a sign as any that Daniel had made things right between them.

As the bruises and the nightmares faded, as their talks grew broader and deeper and more comfortable, Daniel found himself growing quite fond of the master. Coming to appreciate not just the things he did for and gave to Daniel, but also the man himself: his intelligence, his sharp wit, his unbridled generosity, and his willingness to question and reconsider every thought and value in his head. Daniel even came to appreciate the master's large hands, his hair, his smiling eyes, his deceptively gruff exterior and the squishy bits inside it that Daniel suspected he let very few people see. Looking back, he realized he'd been seeing them all along with the way the master treated Jane and Dave, the way he'd tried to include Daniel at his table and his rec room from day one. He'd simply been too afraid to appreciate it then.

When he returned to work, life settled back to normal there, too. He didn't have to see Mr. Foster again, and Tim kept telling him how pleased the master was, how pleased management was, how they all hoped to keep doing business together for many years to come. Daniel hoped so too; if he had to be leased to *someone*, best to a good man who wanted him for more than his body. He tried not to let himself worry about how the expense of keeping him would add up over the years. Tried to remind himself that Carl Whitman's last contract was five years and sixty million dollars, and his star was only growing.

Wrapped in the glow of this newfound peace, this strange quasi friendship and growing trust with the master, Daniel found himself wanting to show his gratitude, to offer at least part of what the master so obviously desired—and, if he were honest, to make sure the master would find him worth the money for years to come. And so it was with only small trepidation that Daniel asked, in bed together exactly two weeks after their first real talk, if they might touch each other.

In hindsight, it was a pretty silly question.

And yet once again, the master surprised him. "Don't," he said as Daniel's hands dipped south, seeking the master's pleasure. Daniel froze, but before even a hint of fear could begin to settle, the master added, "I told you it's supposed to be good, that I'd never, ever hurt you. Let me show you, okay? Let me . . . Let me woo you a little, yeah?" The master leaned in and brushed a kiss against his neck, his bare collarbone, slid a hand down Daniel's torso and cupped his soft cock. "This is for you. Just you. All I want is for you to lie there and enjoy it."

Maybe he was overtired, or maybe he'd forgotten his own warnings and begun to like the man too much, trust too much, feel too safe, too entitled to actually *being* wooed. Or maybe he really was just a terrible slave. Whatever it was, he let his hands fall back to his sides without the slightest sense of concern or obligation, arched into his master's hands and mouth as they chased over every inch of him, leaving pleasure in their wake as he'd not known since—

No. Don't think of him here.

Half an hour later, he came with a grunt into his master's mouth, wondering if there'd ever been a master in all of history who had brought his slave to orgasm and asked for nothing in return.

The next night, Daniel asked if this time, he could touch the master back. He felt no passion, per se, but he truly did want to please the man, to be the good slave such a good master deserved, no matter how the master ultimately decided he felt about slavery. His new request was met with eager enthusiasm, and he tried to match it as the master led them into the shower. Daniel knew how to wash a man, how to make it good, sensual, downright erotic, even; sometimes those ten minutes in the communal shower at the NewWorld dorm were the only ten minutes you'd get with a lover all day, so you learned how to make it look like you were just helping a guy out, washing his back, when in reality you were sharing what touch and affection you could.

Here, with the master, he had nothing to hide, and no ticking clock to rush him through. He thought back to the first shower he and the master had shared, back when he'd been so afraid the master would hurt him, when the master had taken so much care to convince him otherwise. Thought of all the things the master had done for him, and did them for the man in return. Knelt down and ran soapy hands up one calf, then the other, hairy and firm beneath his palms. Then up to the master's thighs, the skin warm and smoother and pale white, so different from the dark skin of Daniel's prior lovers.

But we're not lovers.

Still, there was no denying the arousal tingling in Daniel's groin as his soapy fingers skirted the master's, threading through surprisingly soft pubic hair, but not touching the heavy balls or the cock straining hard toward the master's belly.

On impulse, Daniel leaned forward just a little and kissed the tip.

The master moaned, long and low and in clear disproportion to the amount of stimulation Daniel had provided. Daniel decided he liked that—the implication that the master wanted Daniel to want this too, the same unfamiliar thrill of power he'd felt when the master had asked permission to touch him, when the master had begged *his* forgiveness for wronging him. And more than that, more than his own pleasure, more than that banked, latent fear that the master might grow tired of him one day, find him no longer worth the money and leave him on the market for someone else to lease, he realized he *liked* making the master feel good. That he *did* want this too, wasn't just doing some duty. The man had done so much for him. Was such a *good* man. Even kind of an attractive man, for a middle-aged, desk-bound, rich white guy.

So when the master's hands came to rest on Daniel's head and nudged him, ever-so-slightly, forward again, Daniel went along happily. Kissed the tip of the master's cock again, then followed that with a little lick. It earned him another moan, and still the master's hands on his head were only asking instead of telling, and Daniel answered by opening his mouth and sucking the master down.

All the way down, like his first companion lover had taught him over twenty years back. He could only tolerate it a few seconds without worrying he'd puke, but a few seconds was all it took. The master's hands lifted from Daniel's head and pressed to the tiled walls—so careful not to hurt him, even in the throes of orgasm—and then he grunted and went rigid and still and trusted Daniel to milk him as he spilled down Daniel's throat.

Daniel pulled off, coughing and sputtering but thoroughly pleased with himself, and next he knew, he was on his feet and pressed against the heated tile wall, water beating down on his shoulders as the master knelt down to give all his attention to Daniel's own erection.

It wasn't until they were washed and dried and tucked naked into bed in each other's arms that Daniel realized he hadn't thought of Mr. Foster or the supervisors or his old mistress's clients the entire night.

After that, Daniel spent half an hour or so every night learning what made the master tick, how to excel at what he liked best. And afterward, after the master pleasured Daniel in return, they'd lie together in the dark and talk, and even when Daniel skirted the very edges of the confidentiality clause, he never once feared that his words would get back to NewWorld.

The next few weeks proved their arrangement more than a good one—it was a *happy* one. Daniel often missed his free time, his privacy, but he'd gained a whole host of luxuries and a strange sort of companion—a master who *cared* about him, listened to him, tried as hard to make Daniel happy as Daniel tried to make him happy.

And mostly, Daniel thought he did. But only mostly. The master made no secret of the delights he found in Daniel's hands and mouth, but Daniel knew the man wanted more. Many nights he'd feel a hand snake around, a finger touch lightly where he'd only ever known pain instead of pleasure. He'd stiffen, and the finger would go away, slide back to his balls or his cock, and not return for the next little while.

But each time, Daniel would think about what Mr. Foster had said: *I could've made this nice for you.* And the master, too: *It's supposed to be* good, *Daniel, it's supposed to make you feel good.* They each had reasons to lie, but Daniel was coming to believe that perhaps they hadn't. The master had promised not to hurt him, after all, and he'd proven himself a man of his word, so why would he keep trying unless he really believed . . .

Tonight, Daniel thought. *Tonight, if the master tries again, I will try to let him.*

Daniel came home late. Breaking news had left him chained to the anchor desk until almost eleven, and by the time the car pulled up to his master's house, his eyes felt hot and heavy. He longed for nothing more than a shower and a soft pillow, but when the master met him at the door and swept him up into a kiss, undressing him on the spot between licks, nips, and proclamations about how much he'd missed him, he had no choice but to concede to the master's wishes. Which wasn't to say the man didn't arouse him, even through his exhaustion, because at some point this whole mess of feelings in his heart and head—dampened by his lack of soul or otherwise—had shifted from a sense of duty and a desire to please and into a purer kind of desire. It probably helped that the master knew just how to touch Daniel, just what to do and say to drive him crazy. Daniel supposed he could think of worse obligations to have.

The master pushed him toward the bedroom, and between kisses Daniel felt brave enough to ask, "Shower?"

The master growled into his neck but veered off into the bathroom. Daniel was already naked, and the master ripped his own clothes off, turned on the water, and shoved Daniel inside, up against the heated tile wall. Water pounded them both.

The master pressed a bar of soap into Daniel's hands. "Wash," he said, then dropped to his knees at Daniel's feet and swallowed Daniel's half-formed erection.

Wow, he really *had* missed him.

Daniel moaned, closed his eyes, and let his head tip back against the tile.

"You're not washing," the master mumbled around a mouthful of Daniel's cock.

Daniel gathered up the brainpower to stick one arm out and soap it up. Then the other arm, then his chest. It was awfully hard to do *anything* with his cock down the master's throat, but he squeezed his eyes tighter and imagined that his hands were (Victor's) the master's hands, and suddenly it was easy, it was wonderful, and he ran soapy hands across his belly, his nipples, his face and neck. He was panting hard, knees threatening to unhinge, and when the master held one hand up and said, "Soap," the vibrations shot through Daniel's cock and tore a whimper from his throat. He had to drop one hand to the master's shoulder to stay upright.

The master took the bar and ran soapy hands up and down Daniel's thighs, calves, balls, ass. Fingers approached his crack, brushed along it, and though Daniel tensed momentarily, he remembered his resolution and forced himself to relax, to sink back into the pleasure the master was giving him. He let those fingers wash him, caress him, and as they circled across and around that tight ring of muscle, Daniel exploded into the master's mouth.

The master milked him until the tremors stopped, then stood. "I'm getting too old for this shit," he grumbled, but the satisfied smirk on his face belied the complaint. He moved Daniel under the spray, chased soapy trails with his fingers as the water washed them away.

Daniel wrapped a hand around the master's cock, which was so hard it must have hurt, but the master batted him away.

"Not here," he said, voice rough. He pulled Daniel from the shower, made hasty work of drying them both, and then tugged Daniel into the bedroom.

Daniel needed no prompting to climb into bed. Though his own arousal had been sated, he still had a job to do, and he took pleasure from doing it well. He straddled the master's chest backward and bent down to lave the master's erection with his tongue, cradled his balls. As expected, the master's hands stroked up his back, squeezed his ass.

"Oh yeah," the master panted. "Just like that."

Daniel continued teasing, driving the master toward climax.

Too much teasing, it seemed, for the master moaned, *"Daniel…"* low and plaintive, and Daniel took that as his cue to deep-throat him—a skill he'd still not yet mastered without gagging, but one he felt certain practice would make perfect. Besides, the master seemed to enjoy his practice an awful lot.

As if in confirmation, the master's hands tightened on his ass. Daniel lifted his hips off the master's chest, giving the man's eager hands access to his own cock and balls. He didn't think he could get hard again so soon, but he was at least no longer oversensitive, and he knew the master liked to play.

Daniel pulled back a little to catch his breath, wrapped his hand around the base of the master's cock, and pumped lightly while working the head with his tongue. He was so focused on his task he almost didn't notice the finger sneaking toward his crack again. But now he realized that both the master's hands were on his ass, that one thumb was parting his cheeks and the other was stroking gently over the sensitive skin of his anus. He sucked in a breath, ran his tongue across the master's slit to buy some time, and then, resolve set, freed his mouth and said, "Master?"

Behind him, the master grunted, lifted his head off the pillow, and planted a kiss on Daniel's left butt cheek.

"I, uh …" Daniel swallowed hard, heat flooding his cheeks. He was nervous, embarrassed, more than a little afraid, but he meant to see this through. "I thought maybe … I mean, I know you want …"

Warm hands stroked up his hips, kneaded his lower back. "What is it, Daniel? It's okay, you can ask me for anything. Tell me what you want."

The earnestness in his master's voice was unmistakable. Still, Daniel was glad they weren't face-to-face; he didn't think he could do this if he had to look at the man.

"That night, after—" He didn't have to specify; they both knew what "that night" was. "You said, um, you said it's supposed to feel good. Would you …? I want to be able to do that for you, but I'm—"

Scared to fucking death.

The hands at his lower back moved to his hips and nudged him, urging him around. Reluctantly, he turned to face the master, who opened his arms and invited Daniel inside. The master's face was fond, endlessly patient, maybe even loving, and Daniel pressed his chest to the master's, laid down beside him, and let those large arms wrap around him.

The master pressed a kiss to his temple. "You don't have to do this for me, you know."

Daniel nodded, even though he wasn't so sure. For as good as the man had been to him, he couldn't help wondering how long it'd be before the master got tired of what he had, how long before he decided the cost of keeping him exceeded the return he was getting. And maybe that was unfair, but Daniel *knew* the master wanted more. And he'd been so good to Daniel, so patient and kind and loving; Daniel wanted to give it to him. He trusted the master to show him how.

"I want to," he whispered. "Please."

The master kissed him again, this time on the lips, long and slow and sweet, then pulled back and said, "Okay." He stuck a pillow by Daniel's hip. "Roll over."

Daniel hesitated, trembling.

"Trust me, I promise I'll make it good. I'm not going to— I'm just going to kiss you, okay?"

Daniel nodded. He could handle that.

He rolled onto his belly, situated the pillow beneath his hips, buried his face in his arms, and held his breath. When the master nudged his thighs, he spread his legs, and the master settled between them.

Daniel bit down on his forearm, trying not to hyperventilate, trying not to let his mind flash back to the nightmare with Mr. Foster or, worse, to the nightmare with his old mistress's clients, when a puff of warm air blew over his ass. The master pressed a kiss to one quivering buttock. Then another kiss, lingering and wet, a touch of tongue, and large, firm hands rubbing up the backs of his thighs. No pain, only pleasure, gentleness, care. Daniel kept his focus relentlessly on the present, and even managed to relax a little, to savor the sensations.

The kisses moved slowly toward Daniel's center, the master's hands petting and kneading in the wake of his mouth. When his tongue slipped into Daniel's crack, Daniel gasped, shuddered at the strangeness of it, the remarkable intimacy. He was weirded out, maybe even a little grossed out, but he supposed he'd just washed, after all, and *damn*, but it felt good.

Good, Daniel realized, shocked anew—it felt *good*. Great. Amazing, even. The master made a hard little point of his tongue and pressed the tip inside him, and Daniel gasped again, squirmed beneath the master's hands, moaning his surprise and pleasure. But the tip of the tongue was a tiny thing, and his muscles were squeezing even that; he didn't see how anything more could fit inside without pain.

"Relax," the master muttered into his ass, breath and vibration trilling across his skin. "Just let go, let yourself enjoy it."

The master's tongue drove back inside him, in and out in short little thrusts that sent bright sparks of pleasure from Daniel's backside to his belly, tightening his balls and making him hard again, though he'd come not even thirty minutes before.

"See?" the master said, pride and pleasure in his tone, sliding one hand around Daniel's hips to grasp at his newly formed erection.

"Mmm," was all Daniel could manage, but he thrust his hips into the master's hand to punctuate the statement.

The master chuckled and put his tongue back to work in sync with his hand, reaching out blindly with his other hand for the drawer in the bedside table.

The hand around Daniel's cock disappeared, reappeared a moment later at his crack, cold and slick with lube. One finger circled lightly where the master's tongue had been just moments before, and this time, Daniel was too relaxed, felt too good to tense up. This was *nothing* like what Mr. Foster had done, no rough forcing, only care. The fingertip slid easily inside him, and it felt almost no different from the tongue, just as strange but nearly as good. Daniel let out his held breath on a shuddery moan.

"Okay?" the master asked.

Daniel nodded, and the finger slid in a little farther, and then a little farther still, until it was in all the way.

"Still okay?" the master asked, his free hand rubbing soothing circles on Daniel's back.

Daniel gave a hesitant nod. It was all a little odd, a bit unnervingly intrusive, but not at all uncomfortable, and the spark of pleasure was most assuredly still there, as if that ring of muscle and the flesh beyond it were nothing more than a bundle of nerve endings singing beneath the attention.

The master's finger slid out ever so slightly, then back in again, out and in, and then paused, crooked, and pressed gently toward Daniel's cock from the inside.

Daniel's balls tightened, and the words "Ohmygod I'mgonna—" fell from his lips in a breathy rush.

"Not yet, you're not." The master withdrew his finger and placed a kiss on the tight ring of muscle, flexing of its own accord. "Come on." He sat up, propped some pillows against the headboard, and patted them invitingly. "Roll over and sit up. I want to see your face when I bring you to the most mind-blowing orgasm of your life."

Daniel rushed into position, aroused to distraction and burning with curiosity for what other new sensations the master might wring from him. Plus, the part of him still quivering with fear rather than pleasure, the part that couldn't shake the memory of what Mr. Foster and the supervisors and his mistress's clients had done, felt safer face-to-face with the master, more secure, a little more in control. Even though he knew whatever control he had was only at the master's pleasure.

He leaned against the pillows, and the master put another one under his hips, gently pushed his bent legs wide and his ankles back as far as they'd go. Daniel blushed again, the heat in his lower belly rising all the way to the roots of his hair. He felt so exposed this way, so vulnerable and open.

The master must have sensed his discomfort, for he dropped his hands to Daniel's belly, massaged the tense muscles there until they relaxed. Daniel let his legs fall open a little wider, inviting the master's probing finger back.

The master chuckled and re-slicked his fingers, then pushed one in slowly, brushing over the same spot inside he'd hit before.

"*Jesus*," Daniel breathed, "what are you *doing*?"

The master smiled up at him and did it again. "You like that, eh?" Again, and Daniel moaned his reply, reached out to touch his aching cock but stopped himself when the master shook his head. "It's your prostate, Daniel. You really didn't know?"

"I must've—" Daniel gasped, eyes falling closed and fists curling into the sheets as the master rubbed harder on that magic spot. "I must've been absent from school the day they discussed the intricacies of gay sex."

The master thwapped his leg and snorted. "Smart-ass."

But Daniel was only half-kidding. NewWorld Media schooled all their slaves destined for skilled work, and a companion's work was no doubt more skilled than most.

But then the master rubbed his prostate again and all thoughts of school—sexual or otherwise—ran right out of his head.

The master's finger disappeared, and before Daniel could really begin to miss it, it came back with what he assumed was its neighbor. The stretch was just a touch uncomfortable, and he clenched down, gasping.

The master pulled out immediately. "Did I hurt you?" he asked, so pitiably worried that Daniel was loath to confirm the man's fear.

"No. No, it's fine, it was just . . . Just a little surprising, that's all."

The master's slick hand slid from his ass to his cock and stroked him with agonizing slowness. "Because we can stop if you—"

"No," Daniel breathed. "Really, it's . . . Please. I want to feel—"

Strange, how hard it was to finish that sentence. Daniel's mind flashed back to the basement of NewWorld, overcome with exhaustion and pain, repeating the words Mr. Foster had made him say. But the master was not Mr. Foster, and there was no pain now. Only pleasure.

"I want to feel you inside me," he said. And realized, with wonder, that he actually kind of meant it for its own sake.

The master studied his face for several seconds before nodding once and sliding those two fingers back to his ass, massaging briefly before pressing them inside. There was still a burn, but there was pleasure too, and when those fingers found his prostate again, the one feeling quickly overwhelmed the other until he was left with nothing but the need to stroke himself, to come and come and come until his fucking *ears* leaked.

But the master wouldn't let him touch his cock, and the sensation of teetering on the edge just kept going and going. He was vaguely aware of thrashing, moaning, begging beneath that touch, and when the master added a third finger and then a fourth shortly after, there was no pain at all, only delirious fullness and a freshly amplified sense of impending-but-not-quite orgasm.

"Please," he heard himself saying. "*Please*, Master, I need . . . I need . . ." And God, he really *did* need, would've gone crazy if the man tried to stop now.

A hand touched his belly, his chest, cupped his cheek. "Open your eyes," the master said, his voice full of that strange, squishy gentleness wrapped in the hard edges of hunger, and it was only then that Daniel remembered the master hadn't come yet, had spent all this time paying attention to Daniel instead. "Look at me."

Daniel didn't recall closing his eyes, but clearly he had. He opened them to the master's smiling face, his moist, parted lips, his brown eyes nearly black with desire.

"Eyes on mine, Daniel. Stay focused on me, okay?"

It wasn't a question really, but Daniel found the wherewithal to grunt out, "Yes, Master," anyway. He thought he knew what was coming next, especially when the master hooked Daniel's ankles over his shoulders. Thought he should be afraid, but looking into the master's open face, reeling at the master's fingers working their magic inside him, there was no fear.

Until the fingers pulled away, and the hot, blunt tip of the master's cock replaced them.

"Wait," he breathed, suddenly nervous.

Way, way more than nervous.

The master froze, and the pressure against Daniel's hole disappeared. He could see the frustration, the impatience in his master's face, and added, "I'm sorry, I . . . I'm just—"

"It's okay," the master said, though the words were terribly strained. He teased Daniel with his fingers again, slow and sure, once again chasing the fear away with sharp bolts of pleasure as Daniel marveled once more at the master's attention to his needs and wants. "Look at me, Daniel. Eyes on me. Good, now breathe."

Daniel realized he'd forgotten that. He sucked in a deep breath and stared hard into the master's eyes, seeking strength, seeking calm. Again, he felt the fingers replaced with the master's cockhead, poised and waiting, and after one more breath, he gave the master the slightest of nods, and the master pushed slowly forward.

The head breached him with a minimum of fuss and that same mix of pleasure/pain he'd felt with the second finger. He focused on the one and ruthlessly pushed the other away.

"Look at me, Daniel. At me."

Daniel did as told. The intensity he saw in the master's face, the raw, restrained *need*, was almost frightening. And humbling, too, when he realized the master was *still* holding back for him, waiting for *his* permission to continue. All the times it'd happened, and yet it still never ceased to amaze him, remained a gift every single time that he refused to take for granted.

"I'm okay," Daniel said, though he had to force the words out between heaving breaths. But he really was okay, better than okay, as long as he didn't let his mind wander back to darker times.

Which, *shit,* it just had, and he wanted off, wanted out, but he bit back the panic and stared into the master's eyes, begging him for the one thing he knew would anchor him in the present. "Master, please, I need you to— Please, move."

The master nodded, pushed forward another inch without ever taking his eyes off Daniel, who went tense and then slack with pleasure as the master's cock brushed his prostate.

"More," Daniel breathed, letting his eyes fall closed now that the two of them had connected in a better way, a more primal way, the pleasure of the act allowing no room for black thoughts. The master slid in another inch, then another.

"Touch me, please," Daniel whispered, and a tight, slick fist wrapped around his cock and stroked him deep and slow.

The master matched the rhythm of his hand with his hips, carrying Daniel right back to that razor-thin edge and holding him there, breathless, for so long it became a torture of its own; he couldn't bear it for another second.

"Please, Master!" he cried, and the master thrust harder with hips and hand, so hard the bed slammed into the wall. In a single moment of coherent thought, Daniel marveled at the power of gentle care to take the very same action that had rent him in two with blood and pain and instead have it split him apart with such sublime bliss that he came in a writhing explosion of fireworks and shouts and clenched hands and curled toes and spots that grayed his vision until he could no longer see.

He heard the master's shout a few seconds later, or maybe a few minutes, as he was slowly swimming up from a sea of lethargy and boneless contentment, every last inch of him humming and tingling with bliss. He felt a slight soreness as the master pulled out, but if that was the price for the miracle he'd just experienced, he'd pay it gladly night after night.

The master dropped down beside him, panting and smiling, and pulled him into arms that somehow still had strength enough for the job. Daniel couldn't have fought the embrace if he'd wanted to, as limp and sated as he felt, and when the master leaned in for a kiss, Daniel poured the last of his reserves into kissing him back with all the wonder and joy the man had unleashed within him.

"Fuck," Daniel whispered when they pulled apart, still stunned inarticulate by what had just passed between them.

"Agreed," the master said, chuckling into Daniel's hair.

"No, really. *Fuck*."

The master laughed harder and kissed Daniel again. When he pulled back, Daniel locked eyes with him and said, "Thank you, Master. I mean it; that was … *Thank you*."

But the master didn't say, "You're welcome." He just smiled smugly, kissed Daniel on the tip of the nose, and said, "See?"

And Daniel nodded because he did, he really did see. And sure, this wasn't love—not for him at least—it never could be, not with the imbalance of power between them. But it was definitely the next best thing, the best he'd ever had outside those too-brief months with Victor. And maybe, in another life, in another circumstance, he really *could've* loved Carl, and he didn't doubt for a moment that Carl loved him. And that was enough—*more* than enough for a man like him, more than he ever could've hoped for.

Visit more of the Belonging 'Verse
world with *Counterpunch*.
riptidepublishing.com/titles/counterpunch

Dear Reader,

Thank you for reading Rachel Haimowitz's *Anchored*!

We know your time is precious and you have many, many entertainment options, so it means a lot that you've chosen to spend your time reading. We really hope you enjoyed it.

We'd be honored if you'd consider posting a review—good or bad—on sites like **Amazon, Barnes & Noble, Kobo, Goodreads, Twitter, Facebook, Tumblr,** and your blog or website. We'd also be honored if you told your friends and family about this book. Word of mouth is a book's lifeblood!

For more information on upcoming releases, author interviews, blog tours, contests, giveaways, and more, please sign up for our weekly, spam-free newsletter and visit us around the web:

Newsletter: tinyurl.com/RiptideSignup
Twitter: twitter.com/RiptideBooks
Facebook: facebook.com/RiptidePublishing
Goodreads: tinyurl.com/RiptideOnGoodreads
Tumblr: riptidepublishing.tumblr.com

Thank you so much for Reading the Rainbow!

RiptidePublishing.com

ACKNOWLEDGMENTS

A very special thanks to my very special editor, Sarah Frantz, whose sharp eye and brilliant mind turned this story into something I could be proud of.

ALSO BY
RACHEL HAIMOWITZ

Power Play: Resistance, with Cat Grant
Power Play: Awakening, with Cat Grant
Master Class (Master Class, #1)
SUBlime: Collected Shorts (Master Class, #2)
Counterpoint (Song of the Fallen, #1)
Crescendo (Song of the Fallen, #2)
The Flesh Cartel, with Heidi Belleau
Break and Enter, with Aleksandr Voinov

Coming Soon
Where He Belongs (Belonging, #2)
The Burnt Toast B&B (A Bluewater Bay novel),
with Heidi Belleau

ABOUT
THE AUTHOR

Rachel is an M/M erotic romance author and the Publisher of Riptide Publishing. She's also a sadist with a pesky conscience, shamelessly silly, and quite proudly pervish. Fortunately, all those things make writing a lot more fun for her . . . if not so much for her characters.

When she's not writing about hot guys getting it on (or just plain getting it; her characters rarely escape a story unscathed), she loves to read, hike, camp, sing, perform in community theater, and glue captions to cats. She also has a particular fondness for her very needy dog, her even needier cat, and shouting at kids to get off her lawn.

You can find Rachel at her website, rachelhaimowitz.com, tweeting as @RachelHaimowitz, and on Tumblr at rachelhaimowitz.tumblr.com. She loves to hear from folks, so feel free to drop her a line anytime at metarachel@gmail.com.

Enjoy this book?
Find more modern slave fiction at
RiptidePublishing.com!

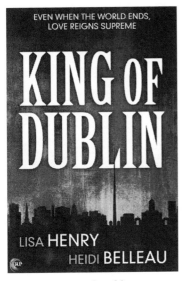

King of Dublin
ISBN: 978-1-62649-096-3

Bliss
ISBN: 978-1-62649-139-7

Earn Bonus Bucks!

Earn 1 Bonus Buck for each dollar you spend. Find out how at RiptidePublishing.com/news/bonus-bucks.

Win Free Ebooks for a Year!

Pre-order coming soon titles directly through our site and you'll receive one entry into a drawing to win free books for a year! Get the details at RiptidePublishing.com/contests.